Love Yourself First

A Novel

Stephanie Thompson

Copyright © 2019 Stephanie Thompson

All rights reserved.

ISBN:9781795599092
Imprint: Independently Published

DEDICATION

To the women and men who struggle with making and keeping themselves a priority. You have a significantly better chance of having what you need and deserve in life when you love and value yourself.

ACKNOWLEDGMENTS

This is a story that I have been writing, without knowing it, during my journey to become the woman I knew I could be. I stand in that place now and want to encourage others along the way.
I thank my children for unwavering support and love. All characters and situations are totally fiction.

1

I opened my eyes, the sun shining through the curtains. I had overslept. I jumped up and went to the bathroom, turned on the shower. "I can't believe he didn't wake me up before he left." I thought to myself. He left for the hospital before dawn. He knew I had an important meeting that morning. I took a quick shower, brushed my teeth, tossed my hair into a reasonable style, put on the spare underwear that I kept in my purse, put back on the same clothes I had worn the day before and left. If I hurried, I could catch the train and make it to my office before the meeting started.

    I barely made it in time to grab my presentation folder and almost run down the hall to the conference room, dropping papers as I rushed. Darren picked them up and asked me if I was okay. I just shook my head. He walked fast putting my papers on top of my folder. I paused, took a deep breath and Darren opened the conference room door. I put my game face on.

    I fell into my chair at my desk when the meeting was over. Relieved. I did not miss a beat. But I knew something had to change. And he had the nerve to text me. "What are you doing tonight?"

He was an emergency room doctor, smart, cool, but with an ego that would drown you out if you let it. I had let him do that to me, keeping me in limbo about our relationship, meeting when he said it was good for him. He didn't feel the same way about me that I felt about him, but he didn't want to let me go either. So, he strung me along.

I stopped answering his calls. It was hard but I knew he was using me. I just stared at the phone when his number showed up. Half wanting to answer and accept whatever excuse he made and half wanting to tell him off. I thought it best to not respond. I had a big project proposal I was working on. I could not afford any more distractions.

After several months, he got the message and stopped trying to contact me. During that time, I focused on my work. I started getting bigger and bigger projects. My boss called me into his office.

"I want to make you the lead designer on the Dashion hotel project. You have what it takes to lead a team. We'll begin submitting proposals in three weeks." He said as if he had no doubt that I could handle the work.

"I appreciate your confidence. I will start on it right away." I said.

"I'll send the files to you this afternoon. Take a few

days to get familiar with the client notes. Darren will continue to be your assistant designer plus two additional designers." He said.

"Okay." I said.

"We'll meet in a week to go over your ideas." He said and stood up to shake my hand.

I shook his hand. "I'll be ready." I said.

I walked out of his office feeling like my life had just changed dramatically in a few minutes.

I was thrilled to have that opportunity at my age. I was 25.

I took the files home and studied them for hours. I googled the hotel chain, memorized their website, almost, and read the reviews. I studied hotels with similar scope and created mood boards to reflect the client's wishes. I had all this ready for my meeting with my boss the next week. Two more weeks and we would be ready to meet with the client to make the proposal.

I went on a couple of dates during that time, fixed up by my co-workers, dinner only. They didn't go anywhere, one was too nice and the other too boring in my book. I think I was subconsciously seeking a challenge.

Two years passed.

Stephanie Thompson

My work was gaining awards and recognition in the design industry. I was content professionally but lonely. I married a man I had known for ten months.

2

I walked down the hall to the conference room, the meeting would start in ten minutes. I took my time, calm, steady. Very different from how I used to be, I was not single and trying to hold on to someone who was not really into me. I had been married for a few months to a man ten years older than me who on good days treated me like a queen.

The executives sat around the large oval table waiting for me to begin, it was our largest account. Their brand was luxury, full scale, with a Bentley available to guests upon request. Their folders, embossed with our logo, were placed on the table before the meeting by the staff.

Darren held the door open for me before every presentation, he didn't have to, but he did anyway, he was my right-hand man, skilled, dedicated, with a keen understanding of the millennial traveler.

I entered the room with a sense of control and contained excitement. I loved giving presentations, the higher the stakes the better. I had been put on a larger stage with total confidence by my boss and my firm.

I had done my homework. It was the major renovation project for the chain's flagship hotel. I knew that a hotel was not just a place to sleep but a destination that had the power to inspire.

That was my goal, to create spaces that uplifted and inspired each guest. I still had those kinds of visions, I was a dreamer. I had worked my way from an internship to the top of the interior design world, competing with famous designers who had been in the business for decades. Long days and a lot of Mountain Dew, my job was my passion.

Celeste Chambers, my mentor, had taught me the ins and outs of the interior design business, how to take a project from concept to installation, the processes and procedures of working with builders and contractors, project management, the keys to meeting deadlines, and how to supervise others. She gave me personal insights too like how to dress, speak, and how to be taken seriously. Lord knows, when I started at the firm, I needed all of that. She was awesome.

I also knew the hospitality design industry, particularly luxury hotel brands.

Love Yourself First

The men in the room, for whatever reason there was no other woman present and no other person of color, acknowledged me as I entered the room.

I walked confidently to the head of the table.

3

After the meeting I went back to my office. Sitting at my desk going over drafts for upcoming projects, my secretary rushed in.

"Deri is on line one. Your mother collapsed. They are transporting her to New York Presbyterian now."

I dropped my pencil and grabbed the phone.

"Is she okay?" I asked Deri anxiously. She was with my mother around the clock, staying with her in an independent living apartment complex in the Flat Iron District. I had been a part of the design team for that facility before I knew I would have to move my mother to New York to be near me. It was a beautiful building that allowed residents freedom to live their everyday lives but with onsite assistance, amenities, activities, and security.

"That's all I know." Deri said. Compassion in her voice.

"She may have had a heart attack; all the signs are there." "I'll meet you at the hospital."

"I'm on my way!"

I reached for my coat and purse. It was freezing outside, gray and blurry.

"Send the car around." I said to Lisa.

I moved fast, scared, my mind racing. I leaned against the wall in the elevator.

Lisa could take care of everything at the office. She was the secretary the first day I started at the firm, when I was one of the new designers. We connected right off the bat. She gave me the inside scoop on everything. Not gossip, but aware. I relaxed in her ability.

The car was waiting under the covered drive in front of my office building, Fitz opened my door and I got into the back seat. Usually I would press a button and the tablet would unfold from the console on my left. I would get a bottle of water from the mini fridge and browse architectural pages on Instagram to unwind after work or catch up on some highly curated news. I was careful what I put into my mind. I liked the cooking and fashion pages too.

But not that day.

"To New York Presbyterian." I said. Gathering myself.

He drove off, cautiously but with urgency, he knew the city well. He had been my personal driver for five years and was a native of New York City. I pulled out my cell phone from my leather bag and called my husband.

"It's serious. Mother is on her way to the hospital."

Love Yourself First

4

I sat in the large dark red chair in the corner of the room, beside it was a small table with a bible and a magazine.

The doctor was discussing my mother's case with the specialist who recently entered the room, the nurse stood close by. I could not hear all they said but the words, "try to keep her comfortable," rang loudly in my ears. I sat motionless, staring at my mother lying quietly in her bed, tubes running to machines. She had not moved or uttered a sound since I got there. It had been two days.

I slept in the chair when sleep found me, a nod here and there, mostly I sat by my mother's bed, holding her hand, gently rubbing her silver hair as tears rolled down my cheeks. I don't know why I cried so. We had never been close. Maybe it was that fact that saddened me. I had loved her from afar because she never let me in. I loved her until doing so was breaking me. Then I pulled away. I didn't want to.

Stephanie Thompson

The nurses came and went through the day and night, angelic in their movements. Comforting. Assuring. But still, I felt alone.

Nothing had prepared me for this. No resolution came. We never fixed the problem. It seemed unfair, there was so much I still didn't know. So much we didn't do together. I didn't want to let go…I grieved what could have been.

I was an only child. We lived in a nice apartment in a co-op building on the Upper East Side. I didn't want for anything, except my mother's attention.

She was not easy to love. Bitterness nearly consumed her. She carried hostility towards that seemed to boil constantly, but she was a master at pretending. It was like she was two people. I always respected her and wanted so much to help her be happy.

Since I left home for college, we maintained a cordial relationship. I respected her role as my mother and I learned from her, how she carried herself in the world. But that was the extent of it. Trying to understand her had left me questioning my own sanity. I gave up a year ago when I moved her to New York. I developed a "just the facts" attitude toward her.

She remained a contradiction. Over the last few years she made veiled complaints about her health, however when I tried to get more information to help her, she shut down. Only after she collapsed while teaching a class did she get serious about her medical care. She had severe heart problems and sky-high blood pressure. She had to decrease her workload significantly and eventually her health was so bad that she had to stop teaching altogether. It was then that I convinced her to move closer to me so I could help care for her.

She remained cold and distant.

I accepted that she had done the best she could. With that I could distance myself from needing something that was not there and do what I had to do to take care of her. She was still a beautiful woman, though I don't believe she ever knew it.

My mother had been a sought-after psychology professor, one of the best in her field. I knew the fathers of psychology before I knew my own father. Something happened between my mother and father shortly after I was born, I saw him twice when I was growing up. I made up the rest, an imaginary man, that gave me something to talk about when my friends talked about their fathers.

I remember that day my mother dropped me off at his front door, gave me a hug and said, "I'll be back in a week, call me if you need me." Not speaking a word to my father, and he didn't say a word to her. They nodded in agreement. I was passed off like a package.

The details were worked out on the phone in brief conversations before my mother allowed the visit. I never knew whose idea it was for me to visit. I never really knew anything with her, I just went along with whatever came up. I saw the visit in the planner that she carried with her everywhere, she left it open on her desk at home. No plans were ever discussed or shared with me. I had had a nanny since I could remember. Shelva. She talked to me.

My father did not look like me. He had straight brown hair and blue eyes. He was white. My mother never showed me a picture. The day I met him for the first time, I wondered if he was really my father. I learned years later that they met in college in Literature class, he was friendly from the beginning offering to be her study partner, actually it was he who needed help in class. He wanted to be near her.

They dated secretly then broke up, his family wasn't having it, they felt he could do better than be with a black person.

They got back together years later and eloped. Though she loved him, she felt the pressure of being in an interracial marriage and would not forgive him for pushing her away because of his parents. He loved her but she could not love him back. They divorced when I was two and she never dated anyone when I was growing up that I knew about. She worked a lot. She went into her room, shut the door, and shut out everything, including me.

 Thank God I had Shelva who was kind and filled in the gap, who kept me together.

 But, still, I wanted my mother.

5

It was Shelva who kissed me goodbye when I started college. She told me everything she knew about New York University, she was proud of being an alumna.

She started working for "Mrs. Bennington", as she called my mother, the year she graduated from NYU. She had been looking for a job in marketing, the last degree she sought after changing her major five times, she could not make up her mind. In the end, marketing seemed a good fit for her and she could use the business classes she had racked up. She always had a plan even if she changed it several times, trying to fit into the role of responsible educated adult. It never fit. She loved children. She loved serving others. She didn't seek status or money, just the opposite, she just wanted to be of service.

When she saw the ad in the newspaper for a nanny, she called the number. She had no idea what a nanny did except for what she'd seen on television or in the movies. The nannies were always taking the little ones to the park and play dates. When the child was older, being the confidant and the go to person for everything from homework to their crush on their classmate. She hoped that the ad was that kind of situation.

It turned out better than she expected she told me later. She said she found me.

My mother had made a noteworthy life for herself, and by that, one for me too. I fell under her umbrella with the elite of New York. Not saying much. Obedient. Quiet. Lonely. Seen but not heard.

Except for Shelva.

She was graceful. She taught me about everything from shampoos and conditioners to how to use the microwave. About the importance of having a few things that were special to me instead of a lot of stuff just to say you have it. She taught me the importance of friendship, that I didn't have to be perfect. The perfection thing was a hard one for me, I didn't know any other way. I stressed myself out. Things had to be a certain way.

Shelva always added a little sunshine to things. A little glitter. That extra sparkle that made the day better.

My mother gave her a schedule each month.

Shelva would break out her neon highlighters and color code the schedule to make sure she didn't miss anything, but it didn't worry her, nothing ever did. She made even the most mundane things short and orderly and fun.

"Do the things you have to do so you can get to the things you want to do." She said and with a wink she went about her business.

She died when she was in her early thirties. I was devastated. It happened during my junior year in college, she had made a point to call me every week just to say hello and chat a few minutes.

It was a head-on collision, a tour bus traveling the wrong-way ran into her car. The bus had little damage and no one else was injured.

I was home from college the weekend of the accident. My mother told me what happened. Then she simply said, "Shelva didn't make it. Her body is at the morgue." I'm going to identify it since her parents won't be able to get here until tomorrow. I think it's better that way anyway."

"Are you okay?" She asked me, pausing as if to take my pulse.

My mother didn't waste time with what she called, "unnecessary" words. To her most words that were not scholarly or scientific were unnecessary. She said in the end words about feelings didn't make a difference. It was a stimulus-response world for her. Cause and effect. The facts were the facts. She did not want me to be the kind of woman who got tied up in her feelings. There was a time and a place for feelings she would say. Limited time. Constructive analysis. Then move on.

Stephanie Thompson

6

I longed for Shelva in that moment in the hospital room as my mother finished her journey.

I felt a flash of anger at her. You could have cared for me once! I thought to myself. What was the purpose in all that you did professionally if you left me behind? Even in your presence, you left me behind.

The tears came like a watershed, I was crying for everything all at once. I couldn't stop. I felt guilty for being angry while my mother lay dying, I was a mix of emotions. I had already forgiven her, the emotions caught me off guard.

I took a tissue from my purse and wiped my wet cheeks. Looking around the room, I thought how quickly life goes by and how important it is to let your loved ones know how you feel about them. Especially your children. I also thought about how important it is to take care of yourself. My mother's condition was a wake-up call for me. Her illness seemed to be as much an emotional condition as it was a heart condition.

I had had a good workout schedule and was careful about what I ate, but since I got married, I had changed my routine. Come to think of it, a lot of my life had changed over the past three months that I had been married. And not for the good.

My phone was vibrating on the table. My texts and voicemails were piling up. I hadn't wanted to communicate with anyone the last few hours. I was coming up for air.

I walked over to the table, picked up my phone and scrolled through the list of voicemails. I stepped outside my mother's room and listened to some of them. All were from concerned friends and coworkers. I decided that I would check the rest later. Deri walked up as I stood outside the room.

"How is she?" She asked, putting her arm around my shoulder. She'd gone home as I stayed with mother.

"About the same." I said.

"You go home and try to get some rest. I'll stay tonight." She said.

"I could use some sleep." I said.

I went back into my mother's room. I rubbed her hand and said a prayer.

"I love you." I whispered near her ear.

I picked up my purse and my tote bag and walked out, giving Deri a kiss on the cheek as I left. Downstairs I called Fitz, he came to the hospital to drive me home.

On the way, I thought about my father. He was an advertising executive, which is about all I knew. I couldn't help wondering about him at times. He should be here now, I thought. He should have been there for her all along.

Two weeks after my seventh birthday was when I visited him for the first time. I had never seen him before, not even a picture.

My mother and he made the same agreement for me to visit the following summer. That was the last time I saw him. I haven't kept in touch because I didn't want to. If he had any real interest, he would have made an effort to be a part of my life.

My mother worked two jobs, teaching full-time at NYU and speaking at conferences on the weekends. She and my father divorced when I was two. She didn't talk about him except with an angry tone and even that was rare. Still, as I got older, I sensed that she still loved him.

Love Yourself First

    I used to imagine that they loved each other and smiled when they were together like my neighbor friend's parents did. I wanted to come home from school and smell cookies baking and my mother give me a big hug, "I'm so glad to see you," my mother would say as she hugged me tight. "How was your day?" Then I would go on and on about the silliest thing that happened at school and she would act interested. "Then what happened?" She would ask. In real life, it was Shelva who greeted me kindly after school each day. Who listened to my smallest details, laughing at the funny things and concerned about any problem I may have had.

7

I was lost in my thoughts like a movie streaming, scene after scene with no ending no connection. Only questions.

    The car pulled into my circular driveway. The house lit up from the inside by the automatic lamps that came on at dusk, looked inviting. But it wasn't. I hated coming home most days and particularly now. My husband refused to allow grieving over anyone.

    Fitz came around and to open my door. I thanked him and said goodnight.

    "I'll see you in the morning." I said.

    He nodded his head kindly, said goodnight and he would see me in the morning. He waited until I was inside before driving away.

    I put my things on the large table in the foyer,

hoping my husband wasn't home so I could avoid conversation.

    I went to our bedroom, got undressed and took a shower. I crawled into bed. I heard him come in shortly after that, I pretended I was sleep.

    The next morning, I went back to the hospital. That time I took an overnight bag.

    Deri was asleep in the large chair that pulled out into a small bed.

    "Good morning." I said softly.

    She slowly roused herself and stretched.

    "This is the most uncomfortable thing I have ever slept in." She said, frowning.

    "I can imagine. It will be my bed tonight." I said.

    "You don't have to do that. I'll be back."

    "No, you stay home tonight. I want to be here."

    "Okay... if you're sure."

I put my bag in the tiny closet. My mother's dress still hanging there from the day she was admitted. She collapsed while she and Deri walked the garden path around the independent living facility. They never walked far or long, just enough for mother to see the flowers.

Stephanie Thompson

I closed the door and walked over to her bedside.

"How is she?" I asked?

"Still no change. She seems to be resting peacefully."

I pulled up a chair quietly beside her bed.

"I'll see you tomorrow." I said quietly to Deri.

"See you tomorrow." She said softly, placing her hand on mine.

I was sitting there when her doctor came, and the specialist, and her nurse. I quietly moved my chair back out of the way and stepped aside so he could check her.

My eyes drifted to the window on the other side of the room. It was snowing, the temperature was dropping. I hoped it would not be a blizzard.

The doctors read her chart and checked her, then talked to each other. When they finished, her primary care physician gave directions to the nurse. He had been our doctor since I was born. My mother told me that when she took me for checkups when I was growing up.

I watched them as they did their work, but that morning they looked somber. They had both known her for years, attending many of her talks at conferences. Everybody seemed to like her. I wish I knew the woman they knew.

I felt empty in that moment, as if I knew what they were about to say.

My mother was the third child of six born in the south in the sixties. Her father had been a mechanic for the local dairy farm, working on all the delivery trucks and equipment. An accident on the job left him with a noticeable limp in his left leg but he didn't make any excuses. He got up early and went to work no matter the weather or trials at home.

He was a decent man with a commitment to his family. He protected them, as much as a black man could protect his family from people who thought you had little or no rights during that time. My grandmother was a quiet woman, gifted in anything craft related. She sewed, gardened, she even did woodwork, carving beautiful ornaments for their home and to sell at the local market. She was an amazing cook according to my mother who managed to share pieces of her childhood during the few times she mentioned her parents. Always the one to withhold information, she gave snippets and I put them together, but I felt there was a big part missing.

The dairy farm was sold when the owners went bankrupt and so was the home my grandparents lived in because the dairy farmer owned it too. It was a small plain unpainted house in the section of town designated for Negros. They paid a small amount for rent each month. There was no indoor toilet and they shared the water pump outside with the other "colored people" in the neighborhood.

My grandparents didn't have a chip on their shoulder or animosity about having to sit at the back of the bus or get the leftovers, or use separate facilities or entrances based on the color of their skin. Not being able to look a white person in the eye or having to ignore abusive behaviors. My mother told me this with a disdain in her voice as if she were transported back to a time that she wished she did not remember.

My grandparents were proud people who believed in an honest day's work. They followed the customs of the day not making trouble. They were respectful and respectable by white and blacks. My grandmother was not in the presence of whites except when she did the laundry for the town doctor. She sang a lot, hummed spirituals. She had met the Lord and believed he was with her, with them.

Both my grandparents picked cotton as sharecroppers, after the dairy farm shut down. They barely broke even, living in poverty for most of their lives but my grandfather wanted his children to have better. He stressed education, at the time a black college that he'd learned about from a neighbor whose daughter had gone off to one.

He wanted their children to go to college. They didn't know how, but they saved pennies to at least help with their bus fare. They had faith. My mother talked fondly about her parents before snapping back to the present and going back into her wall of fortitude.

She did go to college, a historically black college, Spellman. After graduating, she became an instructor there. She eventually earned a graduate degree from NYU and rented an apartment in the Carnegie Hill--- New York City area, where I was raised.

Over the years she advanced and as times and people continued to change, she was hired as an adjunct professor then full-time faculty at NYU. That was her last job. Her memory began to fade, her ability to make presentations suffered to the point that she could not make complete sentences at times. She was experiencing early onset dementia and was unable to teach. She reluctantly stopped working, taking a medical retirement. She was diagnosed with heart disease.

The independent living facility provided stimulating activities, but she wouldn't participate. The only thing she liked was the garden.

Stephanie Thompson

8

She took her last breath. "I'm sorry, the doctor said.

I just stood there. A cascade of emotions.

It was over just like that. Her life. I reached for her hand and held it for a few minutes. Despite it all, she was the strongest woman I knew. I thought I was ready, but I wasn't. I loved her.

The service was small, intimate, just as she had desired. Though she was known and admired by many, she only wanted close friends at her funeral.

I never had children, my husband and I tried, though to tell the truth, I was skeptical. I didn't want to be a mother. I didn't think I had what it took.

I was relieved when I did not conceive.

Her siblings, a younger brother and two older sisters where there, two with major illnesses of their own. Two of her siblings died in childhood.

I barely knew my cousins who accompanied my uncle and aunts, we were never a close family. There was one aunt though who stood out. She was lively with beautiful almost radiant skin and a kind smile. She hugged me and said she hoped I would come to see her soon. She lived in the south near the place where they all grew up.

My husband took one day off, the day of the funeral and seemed agitated as if the funeral was taking away my attention from him. He talked as though he knew everything about death and dying in a matter of fact way. Not showing any emotion and scowling if I did. I was becoming afraid of him.

The bags under my eyes and the slack in my dress showed how little sleep and little food I had had. I didn't have an appetite. I usually ate when I was stressed but for some reason, it was just the opposite that time.

I was exhausted.

My best friends surrounded me. We have been friends since college.

Stephanie Thompson

9

The Amber Hotel project was close to the deadline. I wasn't sure if we would make it. It would be the first deadline that I had missed.

It was a beautiful hotel by the sea in California. Long known as a five-star brand catering to upscale guests. But with the new trends for millennial travelers, they were looking to redesign their brand. I was their first choice to head the interior design work.

The building was almost complete, the furniture and fixtures ordered and on the way. This would be the model for the other hotels in their chain, they wanted to stay loyal to their faithful customers and create a new experience that would attract the younger market.

I was in charge of designing the lobby, restaurant, lounge and bar, and the luxury spa. I had a bonus of designing their rooftop lounge that had one of the most iconic coastal views.

I worked day and night with my team to meet the deadline. During the last leg of the project I was also planning my mother's funeral, trying not to break down. It was the project I dreamed of. I wished I could have postponed it until I got myself together.

I was operating on a wing and a prayer. My mother's passing had taken a toll on me. I know the saying, "she's in a better place" and all that, and I believe that to be true, but it still left me feeling a certain kind of way.

My assistants, Grace, Morton, and Scott worked as many hours as I did. I was blessed to some of the most talented designers in the business on my team. We worked like a well-oiled machine, that's so cliché, we were better than that. Smooth. Flexible. Focused. Full of humor and grit.

They had become good friends too, working over takeout from our favorite late night restaurant.

You can imagine my frustration when the idea of a merger was on the table. Years of work threatened by money. I understood the business side of it, but I also understood who made it all come together. I looked forward to discussing my thoughts with the founding partners in an upcoming meeting about the merger. They were planning to retire in five years and were seeking ways to expand the firm's reach and increase overall profits. But they would consider our input before making the final decision.

I worked while in college, part-time for a huge carpet showroom, answering phones and other clerical stuff. My senior year I got a lucky break. I landed the internship that I wanted, beating out fifty students who also applied.

At the time, the firm was making a mark in hospitality design. I didn't do much designing then, more research and assisting the lead designers with whatever they needed to finish a project. Our supervising designer taught us the importance of getting a firm grip on the fundamentals of interior design. He was an older man and one of the founders of the firm.

He was kind hearted but adhered to the standards of the industry. He led a team of five designers for big projects and was involved in every detail from start to finish. He gave the designers room to work and challenged them to reach their potential, delegating responsibility but he reviewed everything. A space designed by him and his team spoke for itself. He was a great teacher. Working with there, I knew could work anywhere. They were the first to offer me a full-time job during my last week as an intern.

I had several job offers, which I attributed to how

hard I worked and I started looking for jobs at the beginning of my junior of college. I didn't put in applications, but I knew what the top firms were looking for. Throughout my years in college I was active in interior design organizations. It was nothing for me to join design associations, at the student rate, and attend expos and career fairs, getting to know the leaders in the industry.

"Wow! I did it". I said to myself, sitting at my tiny desk in the office that I shared with four other interns.

10

Friendships

Sandra

Sandra was a tall soccer player with a body that most people only imagined having. Everything was in place, the right place. She didn't take herself too seriously, but she took working out seriously. It was her escape. Her chill time.

Interested in business, she fell in love with a business law class in her second year of college and decided she wanted to be a corporate attorney. She majored in business with an emphasis in pre-law. But she changed her mind about going to law school after experiencing anxiety and depression her senior year.

She went to the campus counseling center for help. After her positive experience in counseling, she realized she wanted to help others who suffer from similar conditions.

She remembered that she had felt nervous a lot as a child, and as a teenager thought of harming herself. She said she just didn't want to live as early as thirteen years old. She was bullied in school and her parents fought a lot. She held her feelings in so she wouldn't cause any more problems in her home. She took on the responsibility of keeping things calm at an early age. She was like a little adult.

She did well in school and around the tenth grade discovered her athletic abilities, becoming an outstanding soccer player. The bullying stopped but not until she repeatedly reported them to the teachers. They denied their behavior and the other students were too afraid to speak up. She got into several fights to defend herself.

With the help of a caring coach, she learned how to be assertive on and off the court. She focused more on sports and her studies, and the very students who bullied her later wanted to be her friend. She declined.

She received a full scholarship to college, was on the dean's list, but she still dealt with periods of anxiety and depression. Her senior year it was so severe that she considered dropping out of college. We rallied around her. She was prescribed medication along with therapy, in time, she recovered and thrived.

She used her experiences to advocate for mental health treatment awareness. She didn't like the stigma that went with getting mental health treatment because it often made people not want to seek treatment. Mental health is as important as physical health.

What she thought was a setback in her educational pursuits was only a detour for something greater.

Alex

Alexandria loved the library. Call me "Alex." She said the first day we met. She was an accounting major and already working part-time at a Fortune 500 accounting firm in the city. Her father had gotten her a spot early to make sure she had the best opportunity to be hired on when she graduated. She knew she would. She had unshakable confidence. She was very focused on school and planning for her career, she was sure about what she wanted.

Rochelle

Rochelle was different.

We could count on her to drag us out to "let our hair down."

"Life is to be lived!" She said. Bursting with energy and a fantastic smile.

And,

"Don't take everything so seriously." She said.

School was only a means to an end for her. She studied because she had to. No other reason. You could find her on the beach or by the pool any time she wasn't in class or at work. She had worked for the same women's boutique in the Flat Iron District since high school. As soon as she got out of class she went to work. She loved it.

People came from all over New York to shop at her boutique. We knew it was because of her, she had doubts. She couldn't see her talents…she gave them away.

She could sell something to just about anybody who walked through the door. The customers looked for her.

Her spirit was infectious. Her smile bright. Her hair full of natural curls with professional highlights. Her fashion sense was breezy and cool with quality fabrics that seemed to flow. She was our flow.

Stephanie Thompson

//

Like Sandra, I felt I skipped being a kid. I had felt since a young age that I had to do everything just right. It may have been because my mother excepted nothing less. I think I took on her unrealistic standards. I didn't give myself much room to make mistakes, to enjoy life either for that matter, I was like a robot.

I thought that if I did what I was supposed to do, my life would be perfect. I found out that that's not how it works. Some things you cannot plan for or against. You can prepare but you are not in control. Life happens. It's okay even healthy to make mistakes as long as I was trying. I had to learn that the hard way.

I had a very structured routine, even my free time was scheduled with a to do list. I had to paint my nails at 3:00 on Saturday, clear polish only, they would be dry enough by 4:00. Then I would listen to my favorite music and draw in my art pad until 5:45 when I would put my things away and get ready for dinner. Boring dinner in a quiet dining room with my mother who often read papers during dinner, not saying much.

If I was behind by five minutes for anything, I felt bad. Cutting other activities by minutes to make up the time.

This scheduling did well for my education because I did not waste time, but at a price. I didn't know how to relax. Not for long anyway without thinking I should be doing something more constructive.

That's where Rochelle was a relief for me in college, as if giving me permission to be myself.

"Girl, you work too much!" She said, putting her arm inside mine and pulling me along for some adventure.

We'd get in her old Mercedes that she'd bought from a family friend with some help from her parents. We'd take off like we didn't have a care in the world. In those moments I could see my life as it could be. Free.

Rochelle was determined to make it through college with that old car, as classy as it was back in its day, she never knew if it was going to make it or not. She didn't want to spend any money on another car, she didn't believe in that. She had fun but she saved her money. That was a good thing because she would need it.

We stopped at our favorite Mexican restaurant and ordered margaritas and tacos.

Extra tomatoes and a spoon of guacamole on mine. We talked more than we ate. It was something about that place.

"So, what's his name?" Rochelle asked on one of those days just before tasting the salt on her margarita class.

"Well, what's his name?" Rochelle asked with a smile. She knew I had met someone.

"Girl, you're always in my business." I said. We laughed.

"I know, and you love me for it!"

She was right. Talking to her, no matter the subject was always good because she found an interesting twist to almost everything making it funny.

And she didn't give advice. She asked a lot of questions until you figured out what you needed for yourself. I called it her gift, her ability to mind her own business and show you her concern at the same time. She just wanted people to be happy.

We never had more than one margarita, it took me an hour to drink one. I loved the lime salt on the rim of the glass against the taste of the drink but I was careful not to drink much.

    I enjoyed the laid back vibe of the restaurant more than anything and good company. The music, the décor, the feeling of this too shall pass, whatever the this was. The feeling that everything was alright in the world or would be soon.

    Then there was Boswick Deli near Madison Square Park, close to campus. The four of us met there at least once a week. We laughed, cried, planned, and laughed some more all the way through college.

    My friends were my everything.

They were family.

    After graduation, we went our separate ways jobs wise but not in spirit or connection.

    I decided to take the job in New York with firm where I had worked as an intern my senior year.

Sandra

    After majoring in business, Sandra worked as a camp director in upstate New York. She loved it. She believed that all children deserved the opportunity to just be children, to develop their talents and abilities in a caring environment, to have fun, and experience new things.

Rochelle

Rochelle, with her fun loving self and exceptional work ethic, had been offered a full-time managerial position at the boutique where she worked part-time the whole time she was in college. She gladly accepted.

Alex

Alex had a five figure salary from day one at the accounting firm. A lot of internal connections through her father helped her with that. She told him that she wanted to make it own her own. This caused some tension in their relationship but she was adamant.

She didn't want children or marriage. She wanted a glamourous apartment in a high rise downtown and enough money to spend any way she wanted.

Staying Connected

I was glad that Alex and Rochelle would be nearby. We all kept in touch, calling several times a week, meeting at La Mercerie restaurant a couple of times a month for lunch and for brunch every now and then on Sundays. There were no expectations on getting together, we did when we could. Sandra would join us from time to time because she was farther away.

Our yearly girls' trip was a must do. Those vacations never failed; beautiful places, calm atmosphere, and a lot of fun. One week with our best friends refreshed our spirits, it also steadied us for what life had in store.

Good times or bad.

The first marriage

Sandra was the first to get married.

She met a sexy ex-baseball player who was the director at a nearby camp. They met when the camps came together for events.

They had been dating for about two and a half years when he proposed. They both knew that they wanted to be married around the second year they were together. The conversations were gently centered around that early on, their way of fielding out prospects. They both liked long term committed relationships because they seemed to work better for them than the dating scene.

They were both homebodies for the most part, but they liked outdoor adventures. Hiking, kayaking, biking, rock climbing, that sort of stuff. Sandra said it was unusual for her to find a man who enjoyed the same things she did, wanted a committed relationship… and was so attractive too.

"You're lucky. Blessed actually. That doesn't happen every day." I told her. Of course, she already knew that from experience. She was counting her blessings and so was he.

I admit I was a little jealous. I was striking out, one loser after another. It didn't help that I liked the macho aloof type. It almost seemed like I wanted the one that was the hardest to get for the thrill of it more so than anything. To prove something to myself. Those were the very ones who played games it seemed.

Love Yourself First

I was looking for a strong man. Somehow I equated unavailable with being strong. So strong that he didn't need anybody. I wanted that type of man to keep away the bad guys. To protect me, be my knight in shining armor, I guess. I was in a way afraid of life. Like there was something out there waiting to get me, to pull the rug out from under me. To let me know that I was unlovable after all.

I had this feeling that I wasn't good enough. Oh, I could put on a front, but inside, I was looking for someone to make me happy.

Their wedding was absolutely beautiful. All three of us were there along with her mother, a host of extended family, longtime friends, and coworkers. Her father passed away several years ago.

Alex was her matron of honor. Rochelle and I spread out her train and I wiped her tears so she wouldn't mess up her makeup. She cried happy tears.

They left for their honeymoon, a week of outdoor adventure at a romantic resort in Colorado.

Rochelle

Rochelle opened two more boutiques for her company in nearby areas. She was a laid back manager which sometimes got her in trouble. She had a problem saying no and setting firm boundaries. The lines between friends and subordinates often blurred. This was her biggest challenge.

At times she found herself overextended trying to cover for somebody she should have fired. It was wearing on her. She was that way in relationships too.

After college, I could not count the times Rochelle called me in tears because she didn't know how to let go of a man who clearly did not want to be with her other than sexually.

She kept extending her graciousness until they took it for granted that she would always be there. And most of the time she was. It was usually them who broke it off when they found somebody else. But not until she'd spent nights crying and couldn't sleep, going to work looking like she'd been up all night.

Then he'd call again. "Meet me at this or that place for lunch." He'd say. Off she went. Rescheduling her work to accommodate him.

"He might not call me for lunch again if I put him off." She once told me. She acted like it wasn't bothering her, but it was. She wanted to seem carefree, no strings attached but that really wasn't her.

She was trying to keep him, even if it cost her. Her employees could see her desperation, their respect was dwindling. She started to put off her work to run off to meet him staying up late and drinking was beginning to show in her appearance. She looked tired. If she didn't get a grip, her sales would eventually show it.

Alex

Alex, by then a successful accountant on the fast track to becoming partner at her accounting firm, didn't care much about anyone except herself. So she claimed.

Her heart was as big as any of ours, but she wore a protective attitude that was hard to penetrate. You had to know her. She had to trust you.

She loved her come and go as she wanted to lifestyle. She was single, beautiful, and smart. She had Korean and African American heritage and her family was close on both sides. She adored her nieces and nephews. She stood out as the only one in her family who did not want a family of her own. She was just fine with that.

She owned her three bedroom apartment on the twelfth floor of an upscale new apartment building. She had a maid who came in twice a week and had her meals delivered from her favorite restaurant down the street when she wasn't eating out. She hated to cook and her custom designed kitchen looked like she'd never been in it. She worked late hours, had dinner meetings with clients, and traveled to exotic destinations for business or pleasure.

She liked romance but stayed away from intimacy. One guy, a tall handsome acquisitions lawyer, dared to penetrate her shell. They dated for several months but she broke it off because they were getting too close. The thought of being vulnerable scared her. She was more comfortable calling the shots.

She was still living past hurts. Her heart was broken in college by the guy she had dated since high school. He said he wanted to see other people, out of nowhere. She didn't see it coming. She swore off serious relationships after that.

Second to Get Married

My husband had looked like the kind of man I wanted. Solid. No nonsense. Successful. Strong.

That's why I said "Yes".

I immediately knew I had made a mistake. The day after the courthouse ceremony, one that we rushed through on my lunch break, I knew. He was a different person.

When we dated, he wanted a sexual relationship, I had begun to change my life and was not comfortable with that. He pulled away, I gave in. Looking back, I can see how he manipulated the situation. He probably saw my vulnerability.

My wedding ceremony was nothing special. He decided the day after I told him I didn't want to continue the relationship, that he wanted to marry me that day.   It was the judge and a clerk as a witness. I had a meeting at one o'clock and hurried back to make it. The next day, he should me who he really was.

12

I cried easily. I was sad. I felt uneasy with him. I dreaded going home. I left him after being married for a month. But why did I leave? I thought. He had not hit me. He gave me everything I wanted. What was this uneasiness I felt? Did I expect too much? I talked myself out of it. He apologized. I gave him another chance.

I tried to change myself. To understand him. To be loyal to him. To help him. It was never enough. It was like he was in a perpetual fight within himself. He knew when to turn it on and off. In public he was charming and thoughtful at home he was cold and demanding.

The wondering was draining me. I didn't know who he would be on any given day. The mood swings were destabilizing for me, I was constantly guessing, trying to avoid a trigger. The arguments exhausting. I had to get out.

Love Yourself First

Celeste did not tell me what to do. She was my mentor and had been since the week I was hired at the firm. Celeste Kegan, of Kegan Design Showrooms, which she owned with her husband. She started in the interior design business when women were not partners or owners of firms. She was called a decorator and responsible for the frills and decorative wallpaper of a project, in charge of the resource room with all the samples. When she started she was not taken seriously as a designer, but she proved her skills and lead her company to greater heights. They could not deny her abilities. She became the first female partner at the firm.

When I was in my second year of college, I studied all the major design firms in New York, setting my sights on Briton and Lovure because of Celeste's reputation. After I was hired, I considered myself fortunate to be her last mentee. Nearing retirement, from the job, not from life, not even a little bit, her projects were still among the best around the world.

She was full of spirit and ideas, secure in her knowledge of herself. She didn't start drama and you'd better not start any with her. She spoke her mind, professionally and personally, giving respect as she did it in an amazingly smooth way. Open to anyone who walked through her office door, she was a force to be reckoned with, yet with a grace I hadn't seen before. And this was my mentor, I was blessed.

"You can't take it with you," She joked, about sharing insights with us.

"You can use what I know and take it to the next level." She said more than once.

Seasoned designers in the firm would knock on her door.

"Come in…" She said.

Her dark rimmed glasses sitting prominently on her nose as she reviewed a project. Marking suggested changes and omissions, reconsider this color scheme here or there, in some cases crossing through whole sections of a draft. "Redo" she would scrawl across the top.

Even a redo from Celeste was worth something, it was the start over that was troublesome. That meant you were totally off, totally adrift from what the brand or owner had in mind.

"Go back to your notes from your initial meetings with the client."

"What did they tell you?"

"Your design is the embodiment of their needs, their vision."

"You must remember their needs."

"Interior designing for a client is not the time for you to show your style, but to embrace theirs. Enhance it!" She would say, waving her arm in the air like a paint brush in a bold artist's hand.

Then she might say, "Let's do lunch tomorrow." To let you know that it was work not personal.

It was with Celeste that I first learned of the fire that burned within me, my inner strength. I was passionate about my work, about life, but I kept it hidden as if I had no right to be that strong. Celeste showed me how to accept my power and how to use it for good. How to maintain it. How not to burn myself or bridges with an ego. I learned this from watching her.

She was a work of art. A full figured woman with short black hair full of silver streaks, she pulled one side behind her ear. She wore the same basic colors, beige, black, white, and grey, in some arrangement or another. She liked simplicity. All the pieces elegant, sophisticated, comfortable. She was more interested in the feel of fabric than colors, the quality of the design.

She had five white shirts which she kept hanging in the closet in her office. At a moment's notice, she put on a fresh one for a meeting or a presentation.

She didn't bother with things that didn't interest her and had one thing she hated, surprises. She taught me the importance of a well maintained planner, not as a restriction but as a tool. Preparation was the other gift she gave me.

Prepare. Prepare. Prepare. Until you can give your presentation in the dark.

"Just in case the lights go out." She laughed.

Looking at her empty office, I missed her laugh.

She was that way. Comfortable in her own skin and encouraging others to do the same.

So when I went to her with moist eyes, she listened. She encouraged me.

Then she said, "I don't have enough tissue for you and me!" She handed me the box of tissue.

Seeing a smile and that I was able to take a deep breath, she knew the ice was broken. The ground was tilled. She shared a personal experience, not the same as mine but close enough for me to get the picture.

When she was done, "That's life." She would say. I couldn't help noticing that woven throughout her sharing of her experiences was her faith. An unshakable knowing that she was never alone. That the best was yet to come. That this too shall pass.

She was building me with every interaction, undoubtedly she knew what she was doing, but she never let on to me. For the first time, I knew I was loved. For the first time I felt I would not break.

Sometimes it is another person who is willing to share his or her faith in a practical sense that gives a struggling soul light.

I looked like I had everything, I made it appear that way, but I was a walking shell, hoping no one looked to close. I had a carefully made up outer image. Celeste saw through that and saw something greater.

It never failed, when I walked out of her office, my shoulders were higher. My focus regained. My self-love blossoming. I was getting closer to my own revelations. My self-worth. Undeniable. Unable to be stolen by anyone.

A House is Not a Home

We lived in the same house, but that was all. I could count on him to pay the bills and keep me in a nice lifestyle. But did I still love him?

Stephanie Thompson

We had grown distant over the past two years, practically the entire time we were married, it was like I was married to someone I didn't know.

We used work as an excuse. I was determined to get the biggest design accounts, clinging to my career like a safety net. He worked late and refused to be involved in anything that was important to me.

He was a project manager and a builder, highly skilled with his hands, he could build anything. He was ten years older than me which I initially found attractive, he appeared mature, steady.

We met on the site of a new hotel construction that he was overseeing. Tall, six feet two he once told me, with caramel skin, attractive, more in his confidence than actual looks.

He didn't smile much and ordered his workers around like a drill sergeant. That was my first clue. I ignored it, brushing it off as a man sure of himself.

His work was impeccable, meeting or exceeding deadlines, he ran a right ship. That kind of stuff was attractive to me. I was there for my preliminary walk through of the lobby and spa areas, taking my time seeing what was complete what still needed work, making sure that it matched our specifications. I took notes on my tablet, most of the work was complete.

He entered the room, confidently, in blue jeans

and a white long-sleeved shirt. He wasn't handsome but he had a solid reputation for his work, which I found attractive. He was professional and courteous. He stood and watched me for a while before saying anything.

"How did we do?" He asked. Knowing he had done what I asked for. I liked his pretend humility, knowing that if I said one thing was out of place, he'd take care of it ASAP. That was comforting to her. Looking back, I had a "rescue me" syndrome. From what did I think I needed rescuing, I had no idea.

"Everything looks good so far." I said clearly.

"Let me know if you find anything that we need to work on. ---I'll leave you to finish your walk through." He said and left the room.

I noticed how his jeans fit as he left the room. Not too bad.

He and his crew had done an excellent job, as usual.

I went back to my office. A few days later, he called me and asked me to lunch. I said I was busy. He called a few days later and asked me to lunch again. That time I agreed and we planned to meet at a nearby restaurant.

We had a fast romance if you could call it a romance. More like he took over. I was swept away in that stoic fairytale where he took care of all my needs outside of work. Sending me flowers, buying me dinner and expensive gifts, complimenting me all the time, saying that I was the one he had been waiting for all his life. That he wanted me to be his wife.

He wanted to see me every weekend and a couple of times during the week. I told him I needed some time for myself. He acted like it hurt him, like he didn't know what he would do if he wasn't spending time with me. He said that he wanted to be with me all the time because he loved me so much. I stood my ground, cutting back on how often we saw each other. He continued to pursue me hard.

Then we got married and it all changed.

One day he was swooning over me as we stood before the judge at the courthouse on my lunch break, the very next day, it was like he was saying, you owe me--- you should be glad I chose you. He never said those words but, he acted like a suggestion from me caused him discomfort. As though my part in our marriage was to be seen and not heard until he gave me permission, to please him. It was the weirdest thing I had ever been involved in.

The physical attraction was there but I didn't feel emotionally connected to him anymore. I wasn't respected. I started to hate it when he touched me. Not because the desire wasn't there but I couldn't trust him. Who would he be tomorrow? Or the next minute? I never knew.

    I started pulling away, trying to avoid his gestures for physical intimacy without angering him. At other times, I gave him what he wanted. Then crawled out of bed to take a shower, pull my hair up in a twist and clamp it at the top of my head, get a snack, and read the latest news on my computer. When my eyes were heavy, I went back to bed, he would be sound asleep. I snuggled under the covers on my side of the bed, said a quiet prayer. "Help, I don't know what to do." I prayed to the Lord silently. Eventually, I feel asleep.

    The alarm was an unwelcomed sound. I felt like I had just fallen asleep and it was time to get up and go to work. He was already up showered and dressed. Put together in his customary blue jeans and white or blue button down shirt with his company emblem above the pocket.

    He always looked good, smoothing out every crinkle in his clothes. He posed in front of the mirror checking himself out then came over to give me a kiss goodbye. Having learned by then to just go along with it, I did. Mr. Sincere or Mr. Hateful? That morning, it seemed like he was pretending to be Mr. Sincere, by that evening it might be just the opposite.

    I reluctantly rolled out of bed and with a deep

sigh, I wished I was somewhere else. I wished I had the courage to leave and not come back. I regretted ever being attracted to him in the first place.

I felt like I was carrying a heavy weight. I wanted to stay in bed all day, keep the curtains closed. But, that was not an option, I loved my work and having my own money.

I got a Mountain Dew from the refrigerator, drank it slowly, then got dressed since I'd showered the night before.

I applied moisturizer and light foundation. Eyeliner and lipstick. Brushed out my hair that was still semi straight from my last flat ironing. Refreshed it with the straightener, walked into my closet with wall to wall shelves, more clothes than I could wear. He bought me things after bad nights, his way of making up. I was starting to hate everything that came from him.

I picked an outfit from the things I bought myself. Looking at the shelves of shoes lining the back closet wall, I grabbed a pair of taupe designer pumps and sat on the huge ottoman in the center of my walk-in closet. That closet was my favorite place in the house, as cold as it felt, I never considered it a home.

He had already built the home when we met. But it had very little furniture. He said, "buy whatever furniture you want." When I did, she told me I was irresponsible for spending so much money." I was careful to make wise choices, but nothing was good enough. It was like he picked fights. Only to come back a few hours later overflowing with kindness.

When we talked about marriage when we were dating, he said, "What you make is your money, you won't have to worry about paying for anything." Looking back, that was taking away my independence, my power in the relationship. He would make all the decisions.

It was a forty five hundred square foot home in a gated community. It felt like an island. He criticized my friends and coworkers and even lied on them. He drove a wedge between me and anyone I cared about.

I left him twice before, he wooed me back both times with apologies and tears. Vows to change. Admitting that he had a problem and that he would get help. Until I moved back in.

I went back to him, to that isolated place, trying to make it a home. Trying to please him. Afraid if he didn't want me, maybe I was not really worth it. I can see now how I was running from abandonment issues, not in the physical sense but emotionally.

I didn't need his money, I did well for myself, promotions and opportunities continued to come. I thought of Celeste, my mentor. Not a drop of the wisdom that she shared with me went unused. I was building my courage, planning my next move. I was getting stronger every day.

    I began to read about the cycle of abuse in domestic relationships, the "gas lightening" that causes the victim to second guess themselves, to become unsure, the blaming, the escalation, the eruption of anger, the physical threats that may lead to physical violence, the apologies, the tears, the honeymoon phase. Then the cycle starts all over again. I knew I had to leave. It was just a matter of time before I would get out.

    The sense of control that I admired when we first worked together turned out to be control period. Everything had to be to his liking. His flare ups were notorious. The big things were a breeze for him handle but the small things could cause him to act like he wanted to hit me. The instability kept me off balance. When I tried to avoid a fight, he was pacified. I however, was losing myself more each day. I had almost everything I wanted or he'd buy it. But there was no peace. No predictability. No respect. Why was I still there I asked myself? Why did I think his love as sick as it was, was needed in my life?

Love Yourself First

13

He blew up over the light bulb in the kitchen. "These damn light bulbs! Not worth the money you spend on them!" He threw the box onto the floor after he took the new bulb out. Laying the new bulb on the counter, he reached to the chandelier that hung just above the island. I could see in his face that that was a twenty-four-hour one coming.

He went on those spells of rage where he closed himself off emotionally and any comment from me could spark a fire. A fire within himself that spread to me, with no regard to my wellbeing. I learned to get quiet when I sensed the fire.

The first time that I saw his red eyes and heard the demeaning tone in his voice was at a restaurant when we were dating. I played off what I thought I was seeing, making the excuse that he must be stressed from work or something. He ordered the waitress around like she was there for him only. It was as though he was trying to be confusing to the waitress, to stump her. When she bent over backwards to please him with his menu selections, he seemed comforted. I watched in quiet horror at his responses.

I thought to myself, he is unstable. This man who appeared so calm and strong, was not that at all. But the next minute he was sweet and considerate. Extremely thoughtful and kind, pouring out his deepest feelings, professing his love. He was loyal. He had dreams. Goals. He wanted to spend his life with me.

Nearly every day for two years there were conflicts or arguments over the smallest things. He'd yell at me saying, "You make me talk to you like this!" It was like walking on eggshells trying not to crack them. Trying not to make him angry. I failed miserably. I needed to speak my mind, I couldn't pretend to be dumb just to make him feel good. He said I was using "book smarts" on him.

Having my own thoughts infuriated him. I became afraid of him. Toward the end, I stopped talking for my safety and because I knew I would not be there long.

Love Yourself First

How did I get here? I asked myself.

I could count on one hand how many times my mother hugged me. When she did it was as if she was in a hurry to end it quickly. She was always busy or irritated unless we were at some fancy place and someone was talking to her, then she was all ears, professional, even smiling. At home I was afraid to ask her for help with anything. Her condemnation took something out of me. I couldn't stand it. I wouldn't put myself in that position if I could avoid it.

I worried about everything. I thought for hours, stuck trying to make decisions because they had to be the absolute best decision. I started drinking in high school to calm myself. A friend offered me a drink at another friend's house, if you could call a person who encourages your worst a friend then at that time she was a friend of ours. Fortunately, I developed a different view of friends since then. Back then, I just wanted to be a part of a group, to belong. At first drinking was curiosity and trying to fit in but it turned into a crutch.

Days after that first drink, I remembered how relaxed I felt. I wanted that feeling again. It wasn't a problem at first. I would get an older friend to buy me something with money from my allowance. It didn't take much for me to get that feeling. I began drinking just on the weekends. Then I felt I needed something during the week. I began getting drunk and oversleeping the next day. My head feeling like someone was blasting loud thumping music in my brain. I knew the mornings my mother would be out of town, at some conference or another, and she would have a driver take me to school.

All I had to do was get dressed and slide into the back seat of the car and be driven to the high school. That's all I had to do I'd tell myself, my head still banging from drinking myself to sleep the night before.

It became more difficult to do that. My mind was cloudy, I was having trouble concentrating and my grades were slipping. My clothes looked a mess, I wore an oversized jacket to cover up.

Trying to fix myself up seemed like too much trouble. Getting through the day was my only concern, the minute hand on the clocks at school seemed to be in slow motion. That same driver would pick her up after school and drop me off at home.

At home, I plopped on my bed. Alone in our apartment. My nanny Shelva no longer worked for us since I turned fourteen and my mother felt I could supervise myself. Our refrigerator was stocked with organic meals and frozen vegetables. The pantry with "wholesome" snacks. The schedules on the refrigerator door.

Glad that the day was done, I laid back on my bed knowing I had several hours before my mother got home. This went on for months, at times I would swear off drinking and go about a week without anything but I fell back into it again.

I've got to stop this. I thought. I'm going to get caught. I could not stand to disappoint her, I would never hear the end of it. She'd hold it over my head even as she was preaching self-esteem to others at those conferences.

"You can do better if you want to do better," is the kind of stuff she said around the house. She had no patience for excuses. "A person's choices determine their success in life, make the right choice!" She seemed to have the solution to everything and there I was dying inside and she didn't even know it.

It was too hard for me to stop drinking and it was getting worse. I passed out at a party at a friend's house, a sleepover that turned into an all night party when my friend's parents were gone for the weekend. My friend lied and we did too, telling our parents that the adults would be there the whole time. When I woke up the next morning, I was dizzy. I know boys were there too, but I couldn't remember anything after my first drink that night. That scared me.

When my mother came to pick me up, we were supposed to go to Long Island for an event, my friend

covered for me. "She's in the shower." She said. "We're thinking about going to the mall and having dinner afterward. Do you mind if Yolanda goes with us? My mom and dad can bring her home this evening."
Not suspecting anything, and wanting to get to her event, my mother said that would be okay. I was still in bed with a hangover and no memory of what I had done or not done the night before.

My friend told me that my mother had been there. She bought me a cold towel and I slowly sat up in the bed and started crying. I had started lying, sneaking, hiding. I didn't want to be that way.

"You've got to stop doing this to yourself." My so called friend said. She wasn't any help. Covering up for me and providing liquor. She obviously had a higher tolerance level. However, she ended up in rehab five times before she got sober for good.

I stayed at her house all day, everyone else left around noon. The guys I was told, left after the party around 2:00 a.m. I stepped over empty cups and plates and chips smashed into the carpet. The house was a mess, I helped clean up since I was still hanging around.

That evening her parents returned home, short of a few things out of place, they could not tell what had happened the night before. They took me home.

I went to see the school counselor that Monday during Algebra class. I blurted out everything and that I felt like a loser, that I had drank so much that Friday night that I couldn't remember much about it. I asked for help. The counselor listened without passing judgement. She knew I was a good student. She discussed treatment options and told me she would have to discuss this with my mother. She called her with me sitting there.

With my mother's consent, I began outpatient treatment for substance abuse at a clinic that specialized in working with teenagers. I was able to do my school work while in treatment overseen by the teachers on staff at the facility. It saved me.

After the treatment ended, my mother never spoke of it again. She attended the family sessions but offered little feedback. I continued with after-care at the facility once a week for the rest of that school year.

I put it behind me.

Feeling relieved that I was sober, I threw myself into succeeding in school.

Still wanting to please my mother, my need to please spread to wanting to please my teachers and wanting to impress other people. I didn't know it then, but I had low self-esteem. I was looking for someone to validate me.

I substituted dating for drinking. Looking for someone to erase the loneliness I felt. Someone to distract me from feeling sad.

When I was dating someone, I felt better about myself as long as they were treating me right. Giving me their stamp of approval. I began to feel that was a solution to my sadness. But it led to more problems when I got involved with a boy who obviously did not feel the same way about me but who strung me along. I was heartbroken when I found out he had two other girls feeling the same way I did.

Success in High School

I was a senior in high school and nine out of the twelve awards were given were given to me. My body had changed, developed nicely, I was becoming popular as a respected student with a bright future. Years later my classmates told me that they had admired me. I was so focused on being perfect that I didn't realize how good my life was already. I was seeing through my mother's eyes with her standards. Nothing was good enough.

Love Yourself First

14

At work I was the rock. At home, my shoulders drooped. I felt weighted and anxious. I waited for the other shoe to drop with my husband daily. Sometimes interaction to interaction. Choosing my words carefully, searching for the best words to communicate with him, the best response. Anything could trigger him.

My goal was to have a quiet evening. Some peace.

Then at other times his perception was insightful, inspiring. He could read simple interactions by others like a blueprint that he understood well. Seeing intricate details and nuances that came to life when he pointed them out. He had generosity for strangers with major transgressions. Often showing me how he could see the best in them. But then a woman could press his cereal box by accident as she lifted it while checking him out at the grocery store and he would come home mad, giving a twenty minute anger infused speech about the poor quality of her cashier skills because she squeezed the top of his cereal box to tight. That little dent in the box set him off. He would go far enough as to break down the poor quality of training for the whole grocery store industry.

Then a few days later he is angry because somebody did not show grace and mercy to someone who did something they needed to be held accountable for. He defended destructive behavior that put others at risk saying everybody makes mistakes. But a small honest mistake was catastrophic, unforgivable. It was crazy. If I tried to offer some understanding, some clarity, he'd become more incensed. Accusing me of using my education to make him look less than. That I didn't have a clue how the real world worked, so angry that a large vein in his neck bulged. His eyes widened and red. Pointing his finger in my face aggressively as if to jab me into submission. To punish me for thinking.

Moving On.

My new apartment was on the second floor of a newly renovated building in Carnegie Hill on the Upper East Side. Hardwood floors, a large living room and a modern kitchen with marble countertops and yes, a large walk-in closet. I could see myself entertaining guests, having food catered, board games, laughter. No tiptoeing, no rage. Peace.

It had a large bedroom, an office, a large dining room with a terrace with a great view. If I had had a picture of what I wanted in an apartment, it would surely be that apartment.

The first furniture that I bought was the patio table and chairs. I was paying for everything in cash. I didn't want to owe anybody.

The terrace would be a favorite place under the open sky when it wasn't too cold. I liked apartment living because I wanted to be around other people, to socialize with neighbors, to feel a part of life. No longer isolated. I wanted to be excited again, to do things that brought me joy. I was amazed at what I gave up when I allowed someone else to be the center of my life. Never again.

I sat on the living room floor in the empty apartment, leaning my back against the wall, I took a deep breath and exhaled slowly. Exhaling the foolishness that had been my life for the last two years. I look back and wonder how I made it through, maintaining a heavy work load and designing some beautiful hotels. That was strength. That was determination. That was faith.

Stephanie Thompson

I sat there relaxed in the knowledge of me. All that I was all by myself. I was excited about what the future held. I loved myself. I was making myself a priority, not in a self-centered way but with self-care. Healthy boundaries, incorporating things that supported my well-being physically, mentally, spiritually. I was worth it and for the first time, I knew it. From that place of wholeness, I could love others when I decided to without depleting my resources or expecting anything in return.

I could resume my life, off the rollercoaster.

sat there enjoying the solitude when my phone rang.

"What are you doing?" The cheery voice asked. It was Rochelle.

"I have Alex on the here too. We can't wait to see you!" She said.

"Hey Girl, how are you?" Alex chimed in.

"Good. Yeah...Just sitting her taking it all in."

"We made reservations at La Mercerie. We'll meet you there in an hour."

"I'll be there!"

I looked around my apartment, envisioning where I would place my furniture that would be delivered the next day. I chose my favorite designers, many I had worked with, for my pieces. I was looking forward to the white Italian sofa and the modern gold and glass coffee table and end tables. I wanted a cool sophisticated feeling with a touch of glamor.

About ten minutes had passed. I slowly stood up and stretched my arms. I took the tote with my personal items to the master bathroom to freshen up. It was a sprawling bathroom. A double door separated the dressing area from the rest of the bathroom with its full sized glass shower and sculptured porcelain tube. I put my tote on the sink and reached for my wide toothed comb. My hair was thick and naturally curly. Though I wore it straight when I was working because it was easier for me that way. I got it washed and flat ironed professionally at least twice a month. I did it myself in between hair appointments.

I combed out my full loose curls that bounced back and laid on my shoulders. I wore very little foundation and topped it with loose translucent powder which I loved, it was silky smooth and looked clean and fresh. Some days when I wasn't going into the office, I wore only the powder or no makeup at all just moisturizer. A little eyeliner and a dab of purple lipstick and I was done if I was going out otherwise barefaced was my choice. I picked out a new fuchsia lipstick to brighten up my look, to emphasize newness. Bold. Pretty. Exciting.

The oversized light brown tunic I wore, outlined my shape, it looked good with my dark jeans. My flats were by the door, but for lunch, I felt like heels. My leather wedges were in a box in my bedroom, I grabbed them and walked toward the door.

"I'm ready Fitz." I said to my driver at the other end of my phone. Fitz, short for Fitzgerald is what he went by. He was waiting downstairs to drive me to lunch. The one thing I still splurged on was a car service.

I walked out the door, locking it behind me. My purse hanging from my arm, I reached for my sunglasses and put them on. Big round black sunglasses, I kept a similar pair in each bag I owned.

I walked to the elevator feeling lighter and confident. No worries. No pretending.

At the Restaurant

"Hey!" Alex mouthed and waved excitedly as I entered the restaurant. I waved back and picked up the pace to greet them at the table.

Alex hugged me, we held on to each other for a moment. Tears began to well in her eyes, not sadness, but gratitude. Rochelle joined in. Embracing me. They had waited for me to reemerge, as good friends do when one of them in going through something that only they can work their way out of. I had to come out of the illusion of a marriage. Of what I wanted and what it was. I had to do it in my time, in my own way for it to stick. Nobody's advice would have helped me until I had had enough. Oh, they dropped hints and at times flat out told me I was stupid to stay with him.

There were some lessons that I had to learn that had nothing to do with the marriage or the condition of it. I had a distorted image of myself. I'm not sure where it came from completely, I'm sure my relationship with my mother was part of it, but there was more because I knew other women who had good relationships with their mothers who still struggled with knowing their worth.

My marriage was a symptom of a bigger problem and it was up to me to find the solution. The truth was that I did not know how to love myself. I had given someone else my power.

That's what I had to figure out, the real issue. What was dragging me around like an old toy? Wearing me out on the inside, making me seek my identity in someone else.

Toward the end, pulling me down visibly. My skin started breaking out and I craved sugar. I was becoming addicted to caffeine not to give me that extra boost but to give me a reason to get out of bed. I was either sleeping too much or couldn't go to sleep at all. A day felt like a week.

I thank God for Celeste who had the courage and the lifestyle to point me in the right direction. I began the journey to learn who I was under the mask, the manicured image that I projected so well.

She saw me before I could see myself and was wise enough to reflect me back to be. To show me in our interactions that there was more to me than my job and that was at risk if I continued the path I was on. It would be only a matter of time, maybe years if I was lucky, before burnout would set in. I had too much to offer for that and Celeste wouldn't allow me to go down like that.

Looking back on the years I sat across from her desk or at the big oak table in her office, were healing times for me. I was breathing in oxygen that I had needed since I was a young girl. A safe strength. She helped me tap into my greatness. My true self. My own light. With that hunger for more, I bought books about self-worth, authenticity, motivation. About health and wellness. About personal freedom. I was feeling better each day. Not an easy or quick turnaround, more of a gradual emergence of my true self. I was becoming a force in my own life.

On that Saturday when the house was quiet and I could sense a rumbling in his spirit, a fight about to happen. I stood at the bathroom sink with the warm towel in my hand, opened it out and pressed it gently against my face. I was ready. I had had enough. I would not fight anymore. Not that endless battle. There was no winner. He was battling his own demons. I finally knew I could stand on my own. I left the next day.

I realized that I was dynamic and powerful and loving and generous and independent and whole. I could stand on my own.

The only one missing at lunch was Sandra. She was starting a new week of day camp that day. I knew we would text later.

It was our favorite restaurant in the city, we had a list of great ones that we liked but that one was where we met the most.

"Okay ladies, wipe those tears." Rochelle said.

We sat down. Looking gorgeous I must say. Fabulous. We were beautiful women inside and out. It was like I was seeing out of new eyes, like they had been opened in the most fantastic way.

The waitress came over, "Hello ladies, what will you have to drink this afternoon?"

"I'll have a glass of wine," I'll have a martini,

"I'll have champagne." I said.

We laughed. We caught up. We listened. We encouraged. But most of all, we laughed. Knowing we were there for each other no matter what. That the good times outweighed the bad. That our bond was unbreakable and that made us unbreakable women. Strength in numbers, like minded numbers.

"So, what do you think about your new apartment?" Rochelle asked excitedly.

"It feels good, really good. On my own again. A new day."

I raised my water glass, "To life." I said. They raised their glasses for a toast, "To life." We all sipped our water. Refreshing.

"I'm so happy that you're happy. And back in the city". "We've missed you! I know we see each other once a year but nothing's like our lunches. Girl, we've discussed some things over chicken salad or baked salmon. Rochelle reminisced and laughed.

We were as tight that day as we had been in college but now with more wisdom, hard fought wisdom. Learning along the way, other graceful women lighting the path for us, we stumbled, got back up and moved forward.

Updates

Sandra

Sandra had a successful youth camp with her husband as her business partner. A full service therapeutic camp on one side that offered camps for children with various illnesses, fully staffed with medical personnel and mental health counselors. The other side of the camp was for children who did not have medical concerns. They bought the place from an older couple who had owned it for twenty years who were retiring. Sandra and her husband made some upgrades to the programs and updated the buildings. I was glad to be a part of the renovations.

Alex, Rochelle, and I volunteered our services to the camp during the year, scheduling in two or three days of annual leave a year from our offices to mentor campers or lead workshops. It was our way of giving back, investing in our future. It was as helpful to us as the campers. We each established scholarships for the campers who could not otherwise afford to attend. We believed in Sandra's dream and we knew the value of a helping hand.

Rochelle

Rochelle was by then running four upscale boutiques. She loved it. But, her generous spirit and inability to say no was taking its toll on her. She was the best in the business, but she didn't know that. She constantly second guessed herself and bent over backwards to make someone else shine whether they deserved it or not. She looked like success but she felt like a failure.

Her romantic life was no better. She'd been in relationship after relationship trying to find herself in a man. Which is impossible to do. She was losing weight, bags starting to appear under her beautiful eyes and her bright personality was diminishing. The more she gave away, the worse she felt. She thought love was all encompassing, always putting others needs before her own.

Alex

Alex was flying high on her way to becoming one of the youngest partners at her firm. She loved her work and was fiercely independent, quiet but focused, with no time for foolishness. When she wasn't in the office, she was working out in her private gym or sitting by the exclusive pool in her building, not wanting to be bothered by anybody until she chose to be. She loved her single life.

15

"Since we are being honest, my boss kissed me. I mean a big sloppy wet kiss in his office." Alex blurted out.

Silence. We didn't say a word for what seemed like a minute.

"What?" I asked. What are you talking about? You mean Bart...?" I asked in shock. He had flirted with her on the sly before, but he never touched her. She was used to offhand compliments that were inappropriate that she ignored. She knew he was attracted to her. She did not find him attractive at all. But he did have a nice body and was a powerful man in the company.

He was married with two grown children. He was not her type besides that he was her boss. She would never mess around with her boss.

"We were working late one night and I walked into his office to brief him on the status of an account and he grabbed me by the waste, pulled me to him and landed the biggest juiciest kiss on me. I initially pulled back, I didn't want to initially, but I did. I was flattered. I know it sounds weird but…"

"But?" I interrupted her. I could not imagine an excuse she could tell herself to make that okay.

"You've worked so hard…" I said.

The waitress came with our food. I was losing my appetite. Here Alex was about to make partner and arrogant pompous creep takes advantage of her. She was obviously confused by the whole thing.

"That must have been a powerful kiss." I said.

We ate quietly.

"Well, don't clam up on me now. I know you have something to say. Help me." Alex said.

"Girl, you know what you need to do." I finally said, picking over my salad.

"But he is the most powerful person in the company. Everybody is intimidated by him, he could ruin my career."

"You didn't get where you are making dumb choices so why start now? You're the level headed one." I said.

"I used to be." She said. Now I'm not so sure. I don't want to make it difficult for me by pushing him away. He might retaliate."

"You can't let him harass you like that. Who does he think he is? Grabbing you and kissing you without your permission in his office. That's sexual harassment, you should file a complaint with human resources."

"I know...I don't want to confront him, or make him angry, I can't afford that right now. Who knows how he will react? You see this stuff in the news every day, what you don't see are the women's careers that were destroyed by vindictive aggressors with power.

I just left when it was over and avoided him the next day. But I can't avoid him forever, he's my boss."

Rochelle was unusually quiet and eating like she was starving. She motioned for our waitress.

"I'll have another please." She said raising her glass. It was obvious she was hiding something too.

"Okay ladies, did everybody go crazy while I was in my situation?" I looked at Rochelle.

Since we're spilling the beans, "I let him stay over last night." Rochelle said.

"Who?" Alex beat me to it.

"Kole."

"Doesn't he have a girlfriend? Who is the mother of his child? What is going on here? You two were trying to pull me from the ashes and you're going off the deep end."

"That's what friend are for." Alex said. "We were trying to help you."

We burst into laughter.

My appetite came back. "Any more bread?" I asked.

Journal Note

That night I wrote in the notes section at the back of my planner. I had stopped journaling when I was about ten years old. I can't remember why I stopped.

That night I wrote not as a young girl but as a woman...

Loving yourself is by nature a first thing. How can we love someone else when we don't first love ourselves? It is a fallacy that being unselfish means we must put ourselves last. That doesn't work. It undermines personal development and wholeness. That way of thinking takes a piece of you and misplaces it so that you are forever searching for it in someone or something else. Love of self is the foundation of a healthy life upon which all else that is meaningful to you is built and maintained. You cannot give from an empty vessel.

I closed my planner in confidence. Writing down my thoughts again felt good. I will buy a journal this weekend, I thought.

I knew my friends would work through their situations. Rochelle and Alex had both hit that defining wall that would show them what they are made of. I would be there to help as I could. It was their journey and I believed in them.

Making My New Apartment Home

My furniture arrived around four o'clock the next day.

"Ms. Bennington, Where would you like us to place your items?" The clean cut delivery man asked.

I gave directions for placement of each piece, carefully they filled each room. They were a pleasure to work with, I made a note to send an email to their supervisor saying so.

The whole moving experience had been more than I expected, I was both exhilarated and exhausted. Finally, the last piece of furniture was in place. My accessories were delivered earlier that morning. I didn't pack much when I left that day because I didn't want it. My freedom was the most important thing to me. I could buy what I needed.

I had them put the large ceramic vases on the terrace. Vases were symbolic to me.

"I am the potter, you are the clay." I said quietly, remembering one of the scriptures that I had learned many years ago. That one stuck with me. I was ready to allow God to work in my life. Right there in my apartment I surrendered my life to God trusting He knows what is best for me. I felt a sense of calm come over me. A serenity I had not felt before. I knew I would be okay.

I wanted to restore my spiritual life. It had taken a back seat as my personal life took the front seat.

I wanted to go to church, he didn't. I wanted to socialize with other people of faith, he didn't.

He never talked of faith or made it known to me that he practiced belief in anything but himself. I let his behavior interfere with my spiritual growth, allowing him to influence me. I stopped reading my devotions. I started questioning my faith. During those two years I became more irritable and less giving. Less reliant on my source until things were getting out of hand.

That was when I reminded myself of my source, MY faith and the progress I had made spiritually before I met him. Before him, I had turned my life around. I was seeking God, I had stopped having pre-marital sex, I had developed a strong prayer life, I was a part of a faith based singles group at my church.

He pretended to be spiritual and echoed my beliefs. Only to find out that he was faking all along. He was trying to get me to want him so he said everything I wanted desperately to hear.

Since leaving him and coming to my senses, I had another chance. A chance to regain what I had been building for myself. I knew where my power and joy came from and I was determined to live that way.

I put the small vase with the intricate curved designs on the end table by the sofa. I placed a similar one on the sofa table that was just behind the couch along with a lamp and a stack of books with my bible on top.

I had the sofa placed in the middle of the living room away from the wall with an accent chair and ottoman. On the coffee table I put a wooden tray with a small statue of a woman looking toward heaven, some decorative balls, and a candle.

Love Yourself First

I decided to stop there. I ran a warm bath, put my hair in a high ponytail then wrapped a scarf around it. After my bath I put on the fluffy pajamas I bought just for that occasion. I made my bed and crawled into it.

I was off work for a week to get settled into my new place. I had spent three days in a hotel in Midtown and worked from my room. I was lucky to get my apartment so fast. The owner was a good friend and let me sublet his apartment since he was in Greece for most of the year. He had his things put in storage.

He was a bachelor and world traveler who had not spent a full month in the apartment since he rented it several years ago. He was a dentist with a non-profit organization of medical professionals who provided free medical care to underprivileged children around the world. He met a nurse during his work and fell in love. He seemed really happy.

The week passed and I was ready to go back to work. The divorce was in the works and my apartment was beginning to feel like home.

I was an hour early my first day back, I enjoyed that time alone in the office. I said a quiet prayer in the elevator.

I smiled as I walked down the hall. My hair bouncing, full of body. I had gotten it done Saturday, grateful that my stylist was only half an hour from my new apartment. She had a way of working with my hair to bring out the best, keeping it strong and healthy

Lisa kept up with my schedule and we communicated by text several times when I was off, but to be honest, I was never really off because I enjoyed my work and wanted to stay on top of everything all the time. I didn't consider it work.

She updated me on the status of projects, other important news in our industry, and asked if there was anything I needed her to do for me. She was single and lived in a three bedroom apartment in Midtown with two female roommates. She enjoyed all that New York had to offer, being smart and traveling in pairs, she went wherever she wanted to go. She was originally from Nebraska and set her sights on New York City when she went on a field trip here with her high school class.

She was kind and thoughtful, but she was also driven at work, nothing got past her. She had an associate's degree in business management which she applied skillfully, making our department run smoothly and efficiently. There were six designers on my team. Together we designed some of the top hotels in the country and around the world. We could finish each other's sentences and sit in on meetings for one another if needed without a hiccup.

I took my bag off my shoulder and placed it on

the table near my desk then hung up my coat.

I took a deep breath and exhaled slowly.

I'm back. Yolanda Bennington, I said to myself, looking around my office.

I never changed my name legally. Intuition, I guess.

I walked around to my chair, thumbing through the mail on the corner of my desk. Lisa opened all of my mail and sorted it in order of relevance, taking care of what she could and leaving a sticky not on the ones that needed my attention.

There was nothing pressing in the stack of mail. Interesting but not pressing. I opened my planner on my desktop; the new hotel in Arizona was nearing completion, the spa at the luxury hotel in Hawaii was on track. We had all kinds of gadgets and apps to keep track of our progress and deadlines.

I had an interview the following morning with the leading hospitality design magazine. I liked interview, sharing my experience and the attention it bought to our firm, it was good for business.

The interview was set for ten, a staff meeting at eleven, lunch, carpet samples at one thirty and a meeting with suppliers at three. That was just about my schedule every day. Full to the brim and I had no complaints.

Before, the only thing I didn't like about my job was having to fire someone, but I got over that. I had to fire Rick Shoals after he tried to sabotage my team. He had a problem working under the leadership of a woman. I talked to him about interrupting me during our meetings, interjecting his half-baked assumptions about a design. The second time I wrote him up. The third time, I fired him.

I didn't want to fire him and let his behavior slide at first. I was initially intimidated because he came from a prestigious firm and had more years of experience. But he was obnoxious and overrated, late with his assignments which interfered with progress on projects and constantly made excuses. We were in the process of hiring his replacement.

The last ten minutes of my day was spent quietly going over my schedule for the next day.

I started back exercising at the gym. My membership, had not been used for most of the time I was with my ex. That was about to change.

I went back to my routine, working out every day after work. My car service provided transportation to and from work with a stop at the gym and a restaurant for dinner. I paid a monthly service fee to the Executive Black Car Service and it was worth every penny.

Love Yourself First

My driver waited for me with the car pulled to the entrance of our building with him standing by the rear passenger door.

"Ms. Bennington." He said as usual opening my door.

I alternated between Pilates one day and soul cycling the next at the gym. After a shower I headed to dinner.

Dinner was at Loral's. I was dining alone which I liked doing sometimes, other times I had company, friends or coworkers mostly. I was comfortable with my own company.

Lounge jazz played softly throughout the restaurant, the lights comfortably low. It was a moderately upscale restaurant with some of the best food in the city and the service was excellent.

I ordered a small house salad and grilled chicken. They made the best grilled chicken, well-seasoned and charred a little, a simple meal with a lot of flavor. I swayed gently to the music and I scrolled through Instagram, looking at our page. Thomas, our social media guru, kept our page updated with fresh photos of our completed projects.

From the moment I entered the door of Loral's, the staff greeted me as a special guest. They do that for all the guests, but it was still refreshing.

Stephanie Thompson

I was glad to be back on track with my life. There was something about taking care of myself, making me a priority that energized and inspired me. I felt like I could conquer the world.

I knew it wouldn't be easy starting over, but I was up to the challenge. Even a good change is challenging. I focused on my spiritual development, working out and staying fit, and being a part of something bigger than myself.

16

It had been in the works for several months, talked about for at least two years unofficially. My company was merging with another major design firm. I had been in on the meetings, but I wasn't totally there. It was during the last six months of my marriage. I was more focused on getting my work done well and going home to go to bed.

I took some time to do some research before the meeting about the merger. I got a good handle on the firm's past accomplishments and their upcoming projects. After reviewing their portfolio and accounting statements, the merger seemed like a good fit for us. Just one thing, the personnel. Who was going and who was staying? I would make my vote contingent on my team staying intact. Nothing less.

I went into the board room with the knowledge I'd obtained from my research. I was up to date and ready to discuss the pros and cons. Even though I was a lead designer, I looked out for the people who made the deals happen, assistant designers, office managers, communications staff, those who kept the day to day business running.

I listened to the proposed merger. Our chief financial officer out the cost benefits. The vice president of marketing and public relations laid out the benefits for our overall image and worldwide exposure which would be enhanced further with their track record of quality work. They made good points.

I asked some questions, jotted down a few notes. I asked if I would be able to maintain my entire team. There was a pause. I stated that that is the only way I would vote for the merger explaining that our work was a team effort. Although my name was listed as interior designer, my success depended on the group working together. If we lose anyone of them it would be our competition's gain.

Gavin, the president of the company listened, sitting up in his chair, putting his hands together under his chin as if considering all that I said. I knew he was a fair man and had given me opportunities early on and expressed faith in my abilities.

acknowledged my conclusion...

"We are a team. Everybody goes or no merger, there will be other opportunities if this one does not meet our needs as a company. We'll take everything you all said today into consideration when we outline our response to the proposed merger. "Thank you all for all that you do." Gavin said. We couldn't do what we do without you."

That was the end of that meeting. Three weeks later they made it happen, the acquiring company agreed to our stipulations presented by our founders, my whole team remained intact. We celebrated. Now the work was on with more opportunities, more exposure.

We kept our offices and our building. Only the name changed to show our new image in the world, and we opened a new London headquarters. Gavin asked me if I wanted to head the London office. I told him I would think about it.

It was a win-win merger. There were now two women lead designers. I decided to make her an ally. It worked out well, our strengths complimented each other.

The next three years flew by. I spent two months at a time in Japan, Brazil, London, and Singapore. We designed the interiors of some of the most luxurious hotels in the U. S. and around the world.

Stephanie Thompson

17

I was sitting at the bar in the hotel lounge in Singapore when I met him by chance. I had no intention of meeting anybody much less getting involved.

My career was taking off. I was jet-setting around the globe, meeting fascinating people, and experiencing new cultures. I was living life on my own terms. What did I need a man for? I thought.

We completed the interior of that hotel last week; the grand opening was earlier that day and was a huge success. It was spectacular. Our team had dinner in the hotel restaurant and everybody had either gone to their rooms or went out on the town.

On the way to my room, I stopped by the lounge. All the work we did paid off. I sat at the bar and ordered a lime spritzer. All the full-time employees knew me well by now. I'd spent the past month in

Singapore supervising the project. My firm rented three bungalows for me and two members of my team. We immersed ourselves in the culture, fine dining, and attractions of Singapore. It also allowed us the opportunity to meet and work with local suppliers and craftsman whose products we purchased for the spa, bar and lounge, restaurant, and lobby. It was important to my firm that we used local products and services. The suppliers were also a great resource for sustainable materials produced locally. Our efforts gave the hotel a local flavor that was totally unique to the location.

    I took a sip from my drink and enjoyed the moment. I felt a sense of pride, not egotistical, but a feeling of accomplishment. Job well done. I was just about finished with my spritzer when I noticed a familiar face coming into the bar area. He sat down and ordered a drink. It was Max Worthers, the publisher of the leading travel and leisure magazine.

    He looked at me and caught my eyes. He smiled. I didn't. I didn't know him like that. I knew of him because of his magazine and I had been interviewed several times over the years for it. He said something to the bartender, picked up his drink then slowly walked over to where I was sitting.

    He wore a dark gray fitted suit with no tie and a pale gray shirt that looked crisp even at that late hour. His stomach flat, his shirt and pant waist a seamless flow. He had beautiful dark brown skin.

I knew he was at the hotel for his company's annual conference. He was one of the first to book rooms and meeting space. They made their plans a year in advance and publicized that they would be having their conference at the brand new hotel.

He was considered one of the most eligible bachelors in the U.S. Handsome, smart, and successful. He'd worked his way up from a freelance travel reporter and photographer to president of one of the largest publishing companies in the world. He had never been married with women dropping at his feet.

And there he was sitting alone at the bar. I admit I was intrigued.

I hadn't seriously thought about dating since my divorce. I had no desire to. I went out, usually set up by my friends or coworkers, but no one that I considered a keeper. Not enough in common. The last thing I needed was another headache. At any rate, I wasn't about to get serious with anybody. Work was my joy and my outlet, it had worked for me so far. But tonight was different. As I looked at him, I didn't think of work. That was the last thing on my mind. I sipped my drink again.

"Hello, I'm Max Worthers." He said with his hand extended to me.

"I'm Yolanda." I said, accepting his handshake. I felt like we already knew each other by the amount of interaction our firm had had with his publications. They seemed to feature one of the hotels that we designed on a regular basis. His handshake was firm, his hand smooth, his grip sure but gentle.

"Can I buy you another?" He gestured toward my half empty glass.

"No, I'm good."

"So, you're the mastermind behind this magnificent hotel."

I just looked at him. I knew he was trying to get a conversation started. He was very attractive and I knew a lot about him, but I wasn't interested. The last week of the design installation, my team and I stayed in that hotel. I had a beautiful suite upstairs and I was ready for a long bath and a good night's sleep before catching a flight out tomorrow.

"I've been admiring your work." He said.

"Thank you". I'd learned to accept a compliment without downplaying my work. I did good work. I didn't need anybody to tell me that.

"It was a team effort". I said.

"I know all about teams, that's why I am where I am today"

He was a self-made billionaire and a strategic investor. He bought fledgling magazines and turned them around. I knew that from business media. They were always reporting on his wealth, his financial ranking. I was not impressed. His dating life was also on the cover of entertainment magazines, a story about him sold magazines.

He'd worked hard since he was nineteen, learning the hotel and travel industry inside out. He now had teams, not a team, working for him with offices in all the major cities, at home and internationally. He was the man to know. I was surprised to see him alone that night, he usually traveled with an entourage. I read that he guarded his private life as much as was possible considering his fame. He considered himself a businessman first. A bachelor second, not caught up in the hoopla surrounding it.

I began to loosen up a little. His teeth were so white. His lips perfectly shaped. He smelled like linen with a hint of cologne. He was fresh, everything falling just where it should.

"May I?" He waved his hand toward the seat next to me.

"You may." I said.

He smiled and sat in the seat beside me. On leg out so that I could see his socks and shined shoes. It was a masculine way of sitting, half on the tall chair and half not, one foot resting squarely on the floor. He faced me.

He took a sip of his drink.

"You've been quite busy lately." He said.

"I must say business is good."

"I like the way you infused the local culture into the décor. It's distinctly Singapore. Elegant."

"That was our goal. The community was great."

"How was your conference?" I asked.

"More than I expected." And that's saying a lot. We put on some great events but this one stood out. The synergy was palpable from the first moment. It was dynamic."

"That's good."

"Yeah, he said, nodding his head slightly.

Taking another sip and slowly placing his glass on the bar without making a sound, he said, "Enough about business. We've put in our hours for today."

We both smiled. Knowing the work we'd put in for this moment in our lives, the height of their careers, was years in the making.

"So what's your favorite color?" He asked in an awkward attempt to the change conversation.

"Blue." I said, glad the conversation was shifting, ready to wind down for the night.

"And yours?"

"Green."

"Green as in money?" I asked humorously.

He had a full smile than. It was gorgeous.

"I do like money," he said, but I also like nature and all its green hues.

He was speaking my language now, hues. Playing it cool, I continued the conversation.

"You like nature?"

"Love it. I get out as much as I can."

"And you?"

"The mountains are my favorite. I know this place in Colorado that I visit as often as I can where the mountains seem to touch the sky."

"You must take me there some day". He said.

He was asking for a date.

"I'll let you know the next time I am going that way." Knowing that it would be a long time before I go to Colorado.

"I'll stop what I'm doing and fly there to meet you." Separate rooms of course."

"Of course." I said.

This was the kind of stuff you read about in books I thought. Romance novels. Even though I was not actively looking, I had created a vision board once years ago. If I had a picture of my ideal man, it would be him. That board was long gone and my hopes with it for finding a good man. That was her first mistake. I should have kept that board and my vision alive. When I stopped believing, I lowered my standards, started ignoring red flags. I was surprised how the memories of past relationships came through so clearly in that moment.

I started feeling tense like I was going backwards. A flash of fear flooded my heart. What if this guy is crazy too? Being honest with myself, I acknowledged my fear, and thought it through. That was a just a first meeting, an introduction and a good conversation. Nothing more. I had the power to get to know him at my own pace and halt if I see any signs. I was not a victim. I relaxed again. But it was time for me to wrap it up and head to my room. I had an early flight in the morning.

He must have noticed a change in my demeanor. I was starting to feel defensive, protective of myself.

"It's getting late, I shouldn't be holding you up talking away." He said, trying to regain my attention and warmth.

"Yeah," I said. "It's getting late. My flight leaves pretty early."

"Can I call you sometime?" He asked, not wanting to let that moment get away. He'd seen something in me that he wanted to know more about. He felt connected in some way.

"Here's my card. Let me know if you'd like to talk again." He handed me his business card.

"I'll let you know." I said.

I eased out of my chair, my feet slowly hitting the floor, adjusted my skirt and reached for my purse on the other chair.

Extending my hand, I said, "I look forward to talking to you again."

"It would be my pleasure." He said, shaking my hand. He held it for a couple of seconds, looking in my eyes. Letting me know his attraction.

18

It was well into the early morning hours and still dark outside when I turned the key in the lock at my apartment. I dropped everything in the living room, my luggage would be delivered tomorrow, I bought my carry-on bag with me. I was exhausted because I didn't sleep much on the long flight from Singapore. We traveled on a private jet leased by our firm. I reclined my seat until I was laying back comfortably, with a pillow and cashmere blanket. It was luxury all the way but nothing like my own bed.

    I tied up my hair, took a shower, and went to bed. Tomorrow is Sunday, I thought. With that I closed my eyes and fell asleep. I slept ten hours without waking. I got up leisurely, feeling refreshed. I made a cup of coffee and sat at my table by the terrace. The sun was beaming through the curtains, I opened them to enjoy the view. I was glad to be home.

Stephanie Thompson

That afternoon I walked to the neighborhood bookstore. Carnegie Hill was just close enough to the city to make a good commute but far enough that it felt like I was in a smaller community. It was made up of old classical buildings that were turned into apartments and condos. With tree lined streets, quiet, and near the greatest shopping area in NYC, Madison Avenue; Barney's New York, Dolce & Gabbana, Tom Ford, and more, a host of other upscale and moderately scale stores. Close too was Museum Mile where you could visit the Modern Museum of Art, the Guggenheim, plus two or three other museums.

People didn't move out of apartments in Carnegie Hill often. They were prized locations. I thought about joining the neighborhood association that helped keep the neighborhood looking so nice, but I didn't have the time to really be involved. I donated to their non-profit though, that was the least I could do.

The bookstore was special to me, near enough that I walked on mild days. I had gotten to know the owners and friendly staff by going there every other Sunday afternoon to buy something new to read or just browse the new releases.

I was an avid reader, finishing a book in a few days. I donated my books to a local charity when I was done to pass it forward. After the bookstore I always stopped by the coffee shop for a bagel and fruit juice.

Love Yourself First

Monday I was back in my office.

"What's wrong Rochelle?" I asked after jumping into a conversation about my latest travels. She asked about every trip I took, the food, the culture, how our designs turned out. I was a tradition for us.

But her normal jubilant spirit was not there. I could tell she had been crying. Sniffling as she talked but reluctant to come out and say what she was crying about.

"I'm coming over." I said.

She didn't say anything.

I hung up the phone, wondering what was going on. I called Fitz, he drives an older lady when he is not driving for me. I hoped he would be available since I didn't have service scheduled for that evening. It was after work and my workout at the gym, I had dinner at my apartment that evening. After I made a big salad and watched Bloomberg business news, I called Rochelle. It was about seven thirty.

Fitz was free that evening, he drove me to Rochelle's and said he would wait to take me back home. I was grateful for him always looking out for me.

I got to her building and buzzed her apartment number. She could see me through the video monitor.

"Hey Yolanda," She said pitifully and buzzed me in.

She opened her apartment door, her eyes swollen and red, in pajamas and a robe hanging off her shoulders, her hair barely in a ponytail holder at the top of her head. I stepped in and closed the door. I just hugged her.

We walked to her living room, she plopped on the couch, two empty pregnancy test boxes on her coffee table.

"I'm pregnant." She said then started crying. What am I going to do? I don't know anything about babies.

I was surprised. She had been on the pill since I had known her in college. I put my hand on her knee to show my support. I listened.

She was quiet for a few minutes, staring out the window. Then she said…

"He doesn't want any more kids."

He, I thought to myself, who is "He"?

She must have seen my puzzled look.

"Kole".

"I thought you stopped seeing him."

"He stopped by one night after he and his girlfriend had had an argument. I never planned to have sex with him. But... He said she doesn't understand him, that he was so unhappy... you know all the usual lies, but I was so lonely that night. He left that night and I haven't talked to him since. I felt terrible. I wouldn't answer his texts or calls, he even came by my job. I just wanted to be left alone. I know he's not good for me. Now..." She started to cry again.

I put my arm around her, she laid her head on my shoulder, her chest heaving up and down from the deep cry.

"Like an idiot I changed my pills a few months ago, they didn't work?"

She'd changed her birth control pills because she read somewhere about the ones she was taking were linked to cancer. She must have missed taking them on time.

"What am I going to do?" She said.

"You're going to take care of yourself and this baby." I don't know where those words came from or the confidence I felt saying them but I did. But I was confident.

"When was the last time you ate something?" I asked her.

"I don't know..." I was off yesterday so I just laid on the couch all day, I don't have an appetite."

I sat there looking at her. Not worried at all. But she was a wreck.

"You need to take the shower, you'll feel better." I said gently pulling her arm toward her bedroom. I lead her to the corner of her bed, sit right there, I'll turn the shower on.

She was in the shower a long time.

"You okay?" I said, standing outside the bathroom door.

"Yeah." She said.

A few minutes later she got came out of the bathroom with fresh pajamas and a different robe, a towel wrapped around her head.

"That feels so much better." She said. "Thank you. I don't know how long I would have sat on that couch. Well actually I suppose to go to work tomorrow, the last thing I need to do now is miss work. I need my paycheck."

"You're right I said nodding my head.

She smiled.

I picked up the tissues in the living room,

straightened the pillows on the couch and looked for something to eat in the kitchen. Her refrigerator had bottled water, ketchup and mustard. I called the deli around the corner for a delivery.

"I ordered sandwiches."

"Ok."

She on the sofa. I sat beside her. I'd thrown the empty pregnancy test boxes in the trash. She had the result sticks. I thought she might want to keep them for a little bit.

We sat there for a moment without saying anything. As if trying to arrange the pieces to make some sense of what was happening and how to move forward. After a while, Rochelle said she would just have to make it work.

"I want this baby." She said.

I never thought otherwise. She was the kindest person I knew. She had love for everyone.

"You got this." I said. Looking her in the eyes. "And I got you."

She half smiled.

"Thank you Yolanda. I appreciate you."

"Girl please, you better do the same for me."

We laughed.

The sandwiches arrived. I paid the delivery person and tipped her. We sat at the table in her kitchen, small but chic. Her whole apartment looked like a magazine spread for a sophisticated stylish single woman. Pink, gold, cream, low light, and totally neat.

She lived on the fourth floor of an apartment building in the Flat Iron District not far from the main boutique that she managed. On nice days, she walked to work, other days she took an Uber. Her building had a doorman who looked out for her, just like mine, and there was a nice older couple down the hall who bought her cookies at Christmas and soup if she wasn't feeling well. He was a professor at NYU, and she was a photographer. Rochelle looked out for them too, she'd grown fond of them. The couple didn't have any children.

We sat there eating and talking about doctors. My co-worker had just had a baby. She'd had a healthy pregnancy and a vaginal delivery. She was back at work after a six week of maternity leave. I told Rochelle that I would get the doctor's information.

"He's a jerk." Rochelle said out of nowhere. "That's bad to say about your baby's father, but it's true. I was a fool to get with him."

"You're right. But we've all been fools before." I said.

Love Yourself First

I'd give her a little time to wallow and fuss. Then we would get down to business. The baby was a blessing in disguise for Rochelle.

Stephanie Thompson

19

That summer we went to Myrtle Beach, South Carolina. We stayed on the beach in a brand new exclusive hotel, every room opened to the patio that overlooked the white sand.

    I took a walk on the beach every day we were there. I liked the feel of the warm sand between my toes, carrying my sandals in my hand, my light wrap blowing in the breeze. It was what I had fantasized about, I was living my dreams. Working at my dream job, summer vacations at fabulous places and with my best friends. I didn't think I needed anything else.

    I was at home on the beach, though I would never live anywhere but the city, I enjoyed the laid back lifestyle.

    We all had our own rooms on the same floor

next to each other, getting together for meals and hanging out.

As I walked, I thought of Max and his smile. I hadn't taken him up on his offer to talk again since leaving Singapore. I was beginning to consider it. I kept his card in my wallet. I looked out over the water, the waves crashing to the shore. For a moment I wondered what it would be like to be there with him.

I strolled casually up the long walkway to the restaurant where the girls were holding a table for us. I took my time, breathing in the ocean air, the sun setting gave a warm amber glow to the evening.

"What would you like to drink?" Rochelle asked bubbly. "I'm having a non-alcoholic sangria."

"I think I'll have a... cranberry and lime spritzer." They finished my order. The laugher began.

"You know me so well," I said, tossing my hair back in humor.

We sat at the table and talked for hours. Somewhere in there, the waitress took our orders and we had dinner. The lights were lowered, Caribbean style jazz played in the background. It was perfect, we stayed there until almost two a.m. The restaurant stopped serving food hours ago, but it stayed open until four a.m. with music and drinks.

"I think I'll call it a night." I said, the day finally catching up with me.

We usually took a tour of the town we were visiting, hit a popular attraction, or visit a place that was of interest to one of us. It was a fun part of our trips to go to a place that was special to one of us and hearing them share why it was important to them. These times brought us even closer, we learned more about each other every trip.

We were four incredible women. Beautiful. Spicy. Smart. Successful. Supportive. Kind. We'd become the women we hoped to be through trial and error. With Rochelle's daughter on the way, we were ready to share our blessings and lessons with her. We'd help Rochelle raise her.

We toured the botanical garden. It was fantastic. We walked through the paths lined with gladiolas, marigolds, tulips, ferns, wonderfully large elephant ears, exquisite greenery and beautiful statues. It was a wonderland of landscaped creativity.

Rochelle whipped out her cell phone.

"Wait! Let me get my selfie stick." She said. She was hilarious. She'd gotten past her blues phase when she first found out she was pregnant. She mopped around for days, beating herself up over her situation. It was probably the hormones too. She was miserable for the first three months, but she went to work, to her doctors appoints and took her prenatal vitamins. During her third month, she came out of it and started to look forward to the birth of her child.

She aligned herself with motherhood and didn't look back. She stocked her refrigerator with healthy food, it looked totally different. She worked her regular schedule at the boutique but cut down on the travel between stores, delegating that responsibility to her assistant manager. She had very little morning sickness and continued to do light workouts, approved by her doctor. She was the happiest pregnant woman I had ever seen, and she looked good too.

She was the camera person of our group, with more pictures than she could look at. She catalogued them in neat files on flash drives. A photo file for every trip we'd taken for the last several years. She sent all of us copies.

"Ok, a couple more." We pulled in closer and smiled, genuine smiles.

Our waiter came to the table, "Hello ladies, what can I get you to drink today?" We gave our orders

He bought our drinks, we all had non-alcoholic drinks that day. He took our orders for lunch.

"I think I'll have the special." I said with no idea what the special was. I wanted to try something new.

"That is a superb choice." The waiter said to me as I handed him back the menu.

"And what will you be having this afternoon my lovely lady?" He asked after turning slowly to Rochelle. I don't think he knew she was pregnant by the way he flirted with her. She didn't bite.

"I'd like the snapper and the freshest vegetables you have." She said.

"We have farm fresh zucchini and carrots. How would you like them?"

"Lightly roasted, I like them crisp." She said.

"And for you?" He asked Sandra.

"I'll have the tuna salad and pasta. Some olives on the side please." She said, closing her menu and handing it to him. He placed it under his arm.

Alex was still reading her menu. She lived for a great meal at a nice restaurant, she had this thing about Michelin Star restaurants. She belonged to a meal delivery club that delivered fully prepared meals three times a week to her apartment, she ate out the rest of the time. When she was home, she always set her table, if only for herself. She believed in treating herself well.

She never confronted her boss who kissed her without her permission that evening when they were working late. Although she was flattered that she had the attention of such a powerful man, it made her feel very uncomfortable. She continued to try to avoid him and ignore his coy advances. He transferred her to another building, with a promotion nonetheless. It didn't workout the way she hoped but she wasn't going to let that stop her from doing her job and doing it well. She learned a few things including not being alone with a male at work, no matter who he was.

"Hmmm." She said without looking up. She knew it was her turn.

"The bass sounds great." They were known for their fresh seafood. "But I think I'll have the lobster today." She said.

Sandra and her husband ran a growing youth camp. They had three beautiful children and a lovely home in upstate New York. One of the joys of the trip for me was hearing about her children. She swiped through the pictures telling us what they were up to. She kept them involved in school activities and church allowing them to choose things that they enjoyed.

She only went on girl's trips with us every other year because she and her family vacationed together. Her husband felt it was important for her to go on the trips with us and he kept the kids. If it was a year she didn't go on our trip, she skyped in to see what we were doing. We were just as interested in what her family was doing.

The conversation finally drifted to the end of our vacation. We were flying back home in two days. Tomorrow morning, we had appointments at the spa. They provided complimentary robes and lunch, a great way to end our vacation.

Lela was born four months later. Healthy, beautiful. We all cried. We were a mess. Overjoyed. Grateful. We took turns helping Rochelle at her apartment. The nice couple down the hall and the doorman and his wife looked after her too. Her boss, a divorced mother of five adult children who had become regional director of the boutique chain, sent over a huge basket of baby things and a gift card to her favorite restaurant.

Rochelle was bouncing around a few days after her delivery. We told her to take it easy but she said she felt great, just a little sore. She had a natural birth and was in good physical shape before and during her pregnancy. We went to Yoga class, light yoga, and took walks in the park up until her last week of pregnancy.

One evening a week I set aside to give her a couple of hours to herself. Alex and I rotated each week. We knew how important it was for Rochelle to have time to replenish. At times, we had to insist that she at least go down to the restaurant in her apartment

Love Yourself First

building for dinner or something for a couple of hours. In the long run, it was best for the baby too. A happy healthy balanced mother is the best role model she could have.

20

Max and I had started seeing each other. I'd taken the business card that he gave me from my wallet, the same place it had been since the night we met. I dialed the number a little scared. He'd given me his office number that rings at his executive assistant's desk. He had told her that no matter where he was, to put me through to him. He later told me that he gave me his office number instead of his personal number because he didn't want to seem too forward that night.

"Hello," He answered.

"Hello Max." I said. Glad to hear his voice.

"You don't know how many times I've hoped it was you calling. If you would have taken any longer, I would have called you and took my chances."

"I've had a lot going on." I said.

How are you?" He asked.

"I'm good. And you?"

That was the beginning of us talking by phone often. Then we met for lunch or dinner, when we were both in town. My schedule stayed full and I traveled several times a year for projects.

Max liked to cook, and he was good at it, I was just learning how to. I invited him to join me for a couple of cooking classes where we ate the dinner we cooked. It was a fun.

He had a gorgeous apartment in a new high-rise in Midtown, large with an open floor plan and a large chef's kitchen. He made dinner a few times, I helped him prepare, chopping vegetables and things like that.

His headquarters was in Los Angeles with offices in New York. He was either in town on business or flew in to spend time with me. He had an apartment in LA and New York, and a home in London. He was beginning to spend more time in New York and arranging more business meetings there.

I started to trust him more and stopped waiting for the other shoe to drop that would reveal he was not what he pretended to be. It didn't happen. His flaw was that he worked all the time, not unlike me. He was interested in what interested me, I felt the same way about his pursuits and hobbies. We rooted for each other. He listened to my concerns. He adored my friends. He and Sandra's husband bonded over the love of baseball.

    I enjoyed his company, his friendship. But I didn't need it. What I'm saying is that he was a great addition to my already full life. In the past I had either been dependent on someone to make me happy or a stone wall fortress not letting anybody in. Max was slowly bringing me to the center. I was bringing him a sense of family, something he had been missing for a long time.

    We were seeing each other for months before we kissed. He had a magnificent kiss. His lips the perfect size, his breath fresh. He applied the right amount of pressure and released to my lips with smooth gentleness. I was melting. We didn't go any further than that because we wanted to know each other without the complication that might come from being sexually intimate. We spent many nights in each other's arms on his couch or mine watching movies or talking. We both liked jazz, I preferred smooth, he liked old school.

    Saturdays we spent at the park, Bryant or Central, or the High Line, walking and talking. We walked arm in arm or just walked close to each other. I could tell he was taking it slow. He was smart because I was not in a hurry.

Love Yourself First

He went with me to my favorite bookstore on Sunday afternoons, browsing the aisles and reading book jackets. He even bought a few. He was into historical fiction but confessed he hadn't read a whole book in a long time because he liked podcasts better. He was used to putting on his headphones on flights or after work and listening to the latest podcasts on business or finance.

After the bookstore, we'd have hot sandwiches at the deli and stroll back to my apartment. I invited him in, we'd watch a movie, sometimes two.

It was like we were both allowing each other time to enjoy being together without pressure. It worked. I fell in love with him.

We dated for two years. He proposed on the Bow Bridge on a beautiful fall day in Central Park. I said yes. He got up off his knee and we kissed. I held his face in my hands, he held me in his arms.

We got married the following fall on the beach at a five-star hotel in Italy on Lake Como. I wore a custom-made sculpted Vera Wang gown that draped my shape. He wore a tailored sand colored suit that showed how fine he was, is. His gorgeous smile. His love. His friendship. His sense of humor. I looked at him as we stood at the altar, he held my hand in his. We read our handwritten vows. It was the best day of my life.

Stephanie Thompson

We danced away the evening. All our friends there with us. We started our life together. I had learned to love myself first. After that, the rest took care of itself.

ABOUT THE AUTHOR

Stephanie is a native of Emerson, Arkansas who dreamed of living in New York as a teenager. This is the fourth book she has written and her first novel. She is a graduate of Southern Arkansas University in Magnolia with a master's degree in Counseling. She is a wife and the mother of two wonderful children. She currently lives in Hot Springs, Arkansas and writes full-time.

Made in the USA
Coppell, TX
15 February 2020